F

Sinn

New *X Rated* titles from *X Libris*:

Game of Masks	Roxanne Morgan
Acting It Out	Vanessa Davies
Private Act	Zara Devereux
Who Dares Sins	Roxanne Morgan
The Dominatrix	Emma Allan
House of Decadence	Lucia Cubelli

The *X Libris* series:

Arousing Anna	Nina Sheridan
The Women's Club	Vanessa Davies
Velvet Touch	Zara Devereux
The Gambler	Tallulah Sharpe
Forbidden Desires	Marina Anderson
Letting Go	Cathy Hunter
Two Women	Emma Allan
Pleasure Bound	Susan Swann
Silken Bonds	Zara Devereux
Rough Trade	Emma Allan
Cirque Erotique	Mikki Leone
Lessons in Lust	Emma Allan
Lottery Lovers	Vanessa Davies
Overexposed	Ginnie Bond
G-Strings	Stephanie Ash
Black Stockings	Emma Allan
Perfect Partners	Natalie Blake
Legacy of Desire	Marina Anderson
Searching for Sex	Emma Allan
Private Parties	Stephanie Ash
Sin and Seduction	Emma Allan

Sinner Takes All

Roxanne Morgan

X
RATED

An *X Libris* Book

First published as *Bets* by X Libris in 1997
This edition published in 2000

Copyright © Roxanne Morgan 1997

The moral right of the author has been asserted.

A CIP catalogue record for this book
is available from the British Library.

ISBN 0 7515 3073 5

Typeset by
Derek Doyle & Associates, Liverpool
Printed and bound in Great Britain by
Clays Ltd, St Ives plc

X Libris
A Division of
Little, Brown and Company (UK)
Brettenham House
Lancaster Place
London WC2E 7EN

The Lady Roxanne dedicates this book to her friends who helped her with advice and research. Particularly for Chapter Eight . . .

Chapter One

AT THE EXACT moment that Shannon Garrett came, the audience began to applaud her.

A single spotlight illuminated the stage. The theatre filled with cheering.

'Ohh!' Shudders of pleasure ran through her flesh. Heat flushed her skin. She slapped her hands down on her thighs, trapping the young man's hands where he was gripping her. The actor's hands were hard and strong. His firm belly pressed up against her inner thighs. He held her up, her toes barely touching the floor, her back pressed against a hard surface.

'Again!' she gasped.

The ripple of applause died down quickly. A hush of anticipation descended. The main body of the hall was a velvet blackness. Shannon's head tilted back. Above, a few candles made the wooden rails of the galleries gleam. Galleries on three sides of her, going up into the darkness, three or four storeys high. From the gallery seats Shannon caught the glint of candlelight from rings, from watches, from the eyes of the hundreds of faces looking down at her.

She felt no urge to question. The demands of her flesh were too imperative.

She lowered her head slowly, languorously. She lifted her hands and wound the man's long brown curls between her fingers. Her hands clenched.

'Take me again!' she growled.

The man's head dipped, and he buried his lips against her bare shoulders. His cock remained rigid, jammed up her, filling her to the brim. Shannon tried to raise herself and look down to see it, but the frothing mass of her satin skirts blocked her view.

He moved inside her.

His linen shirt with its lace collar hung open. Sweat shone on his chest. The warm, sweet smell of sex and bodies filled her nostrils. Patchouli scent drifted down from the wings. The cock inside her thrust up, up, *up*, and she gasped. The man drew it back until the thick head of his glans teased the lips of her vagina.

'More?' His smile was crooked, appealing, and wide. His face dripped sweat. 'More, sweetheart?'

'Yes!' There *was* something hard pressing up against her back. Something hard and narrow. The wooden pillar of a four-poster bed. The bed curtains were drawn back in red velvet swathes, disclosing the bed fully to the audience.

In their full view, she slid her hand down under her skirts. The wiry hair on his belly brushed her hand. Her fingers sought his plump, firm prick. She gripped the velvet hardness.

She began slowly to rub the sheath of skin back and forth over his glans. She heard him gasp. She wound one leg around his for support. The tough cloth of his breeches and the soft leather of his boots

2

slid against her calf and thigh. Her body felt every weave of the cotton. Her toes slid across the wrinkled leather of his boots. She gripped his cock hard.

'Now!' She let go of him, shifted her weight and slid back down on to the lace-fringed linen pillows that were piled high on the bed itself.

He fell with her as she pulled him down on top of her.

She licked at his shoulder. His sweat was salt. The softness of his shoulder-length hair brushed across her face. She caught the glint of an earring in his ear. His welcome weight pressed her down on to the bed, down among the soft pillows that cushioned her back. She felt his rapid breathing as his chest rose and fell against hers.

Her groin throbbed. She thrust her hips up against him and he gasped. A ripple of applause broke the hushed silence and someone called 'Yes!' from the dark auditorium.

'Ah, now.' Not so fast . . .' The man raised himself up. His strong hands gripped her bare shoulders. His palms rasped against her skin. She flinched with sheer overload of sensation. He reached for the top of her jewelled, laced bodice. With one sharp movement he ripped it down. She heard a seam tear. The tight cloth pinned her upper arms to her sides and pushed her breasts up, swelling, to his waiting mouth.

Shannon gasped. She couldn't move. His tongue caressed her exposed nipples which jutted into the cold air of the theatre. They hardened instantly. She thrashed her legs in the confining gown. His hard thighs pushed between hers, the tip of his cock teasing her.

With one hand, the man eased her breasts out of

3

her dress, cupping their firm, swelling bulk. He squeezed her taut flesh. His wet, hot tongue traced up the curve of one breast, up over her collarbone, up the smooth skin of her throat, to her mouth. Her lips opened. His mouth fastened bruisingly hard on hers. His hot tongue thrust into her mouth. She felt her fullness and relished it.

'Yes!' She flung her arms around him. She embraced his wide, muscled shoulders. His shirt was wringing wet, and his flesh burning hot. Her hands made claws and dug into his back.

He tore his mouth away. 'Yes! Now!'

Her hips arched up. Her sex ached for his thrust. Her lacy undergarments slid down her thighs to the stage floor. The applause began again. She could think of nothing but his body.

His hips pounded down. She spread her legs wide. The tip of his cock thrust her labia apart and the thick bulk rammed up into her, pushing her apart, thrusting again, thrusting *again*—

Shannon's body arched. She cried out. A flood of hot pleasure pulsed through her body from her sex. She came again, and, riding the thrust of his still-hard cock, came for a third time. The applause became thunderous.

She sprawled back, breath hissing from her throat. The audience cheered. Sated pleasure relaxed every muscle in her body. The thin cotton of her lacy petticoat clung to her thighs, soaked with sweat . . .

BRRRRRRRRRRRRRRRRRRRRRRRRRRRRRRRRRRRRRRR!

'*What?*' Shannon yelped.

The siren – or was it a bell? – drowned out her voice. She tried to shout.

4

BRRRRRRRRRRRRRRRRRRRRRRRRRRRR
RRRRRRRRRRR!!

The noise ripped through the theatre again. A fire alarm? The end of the world? She thrashed, tangled in something.

Tangled in a duvet.

The cover of a duvet soaked with sweat.

The sun blared through the hotel bedroom window directly into her eyes.

'Oh, what?' Shannon Garrett groaned as she finally woke up. There was no man beside her. The hotel bed was empty.

The harsh fire alarm became the buzzing of her travel alarm clock. Shannon whimpered. She slammed her hand down on the doze button.

'Why am I *doing* this?' She paused. There was no one in the hotel bedroom with her. She continued to address (for want of an audience) the ceiling. 'Why am I not doing *that*?'

There had been a time when she had engaged in sexual adventures not that far short of this morning's dream. It had not even been long ago. Eighteen months, maybe; two years at the most. But since then . . .

The alarm clock shrilled again. Shannon jumped. The pleasurable half-doze vanished. She looked at the green digital read-out. 05:30. Five-thirty in the morning.

That's why I'm not doing this any more. Because I'm working thirty-six hours a day! Because I have to get up and practise my sales presentation for this conference. Oh, shit.

Shannon Garrett sat up in bed. She slept naked, as always. Her smooth shoulders and full rounded breasts were slick with sweat from the dream. Her

5

curly auburn-brown hair stuck to her cheek. She swept it back. Her grey-green eyes screwed up against the morning light. A sharp pain dug in above one brow.

I certainly shouldn't have drunk those last four daiquiris, she thought despairingly. It's five-thirty in the morning. I am in a hotel in Luton. I have a sales presentation for *Femme* magazine. I feel like death. I would much rather be at home, waking up around ten – or rather, being woken up around ten by a large, muscular young man with a hard-on . . .

But *Femme*'s worth it. I finally made editor. It's *my* magazine now.

Shannon dropped the duvet, swung her feet over the side of the bed and stood up. The wardrobe mirror reflected the soft, easy lines of her body: her smooth hips, her long, strong legs.

Her dream vanished. A memory began suddenly to surface.

I didn't.

Oh God, I *didn't*.

I can't have!

Shannon sat down again on the bed, cradling her throbbing head in her hands.

Oh yes I did, she thought. Shannon Garrett puts her foot in it again – *right* in it! I can't believe I let Richard Stanley even start a conversation with me, never mind anything else!

Shannon sat in the morning sun. The early heat poured over her skin like warm cream. She raised her eyes to the window with a gaze that saw nothing of the sparkling dawn skies.

'Just *what* have I agreed to?' she implored the empty room.

6

Her mind raced frantically back to the night before . . .

Chapter Two

... *AND RICHARD STANLEY.*

Richard leaned back against the plush hotel bar seat. His well-cut blond hair was unruffled. His suit was not even wrinkled. And it was past two in the morning, and the day had been crammed full of meetings. His eyes were only a little red. Damn, Shannon thought. How does he do that?

She eased her high-heeled shoes off, under cover of the table.

'So anyway,' Richard Stanley continued, 'this girl I knew worked for a telephone sex-line. You know: for sad gits who can't get a bird. And perverts. Geeks who like sniffing panties.'

There was a snicker from the gathered editors and editorial assistants employed by the various branches of Midnight Rose International. Most of the group who had stayed the course in the bar tonight were male. Shannon fixed Richard with a sharp (if rather glassy) stare. She sipped her daiquiri.

Richard leaned forward into the centre of the group. He whispered conspiratorially. 'And you know what? She ended up in the mail-order business. She told me she made more money selling her used panties to dirty old men than she did on the phone lines!'

A secretary from *Babes!* went, 'Ick! That's disgusting!'

Shannon Garrett did not like the staff that Richard collected around him on *Babes!* magazine. Come to think of it, she told herself, I don't like him, I don't like his magazine, I don't like his people, and I certainly don't like men who use schoolboy stories to gross out the women they work with.

And just because *Femme* and *Babes!* are both owned by Midnight Rose International, that doesn't mean I have to be nice to him.

Especially when he thinks he can be more disgusting than a woman . . .

'Used panties are easy money,' Shannon said off-handedly. 'I had a friend in the business, once. She tells me it can be faked convincingly with anchovy paste and tuna.'

This time the 'ick!' was general. Shannon grinned.

There was a glint in Richard's pale blue, faintly bloodshot eyes that made Shannon think he wasn't as sober as he looked. 'You'd know all about faking it,' he murmured smoothly.

Shannon gritted her teeth. Then she smiled. 'And you'd know all about sad perverts.'

'How about it's my round?' Gary interrupted. He was one of Shannon's editorial assistants: a lithe young twenty-two-year-old with one earring and a cheeky grin. He deliberately leaned between Shannon and Richard to collect their glasses. He murmured, 'Save the blood on the carpet for

9

tomorrow's meeting, yeah?'

'Yes,' Shannon muttered. Her rival editor, Richard, said nothing. She added, deliberately provocatively, 'After all, since *Babes!* is going to be deep-sixed, I suppose we should all be kind to Richard . . .'

Gary shrugged and went to the bar. He wore a helpless grin. Richard Stanley leaned his arms on the polished wooden surface of the table and brought his face closer to Shannon.

Richard's breath smelled of alcohol. 'Somehow, sweetheart, I don't think *my* magazine is the one that's going to be cancelled. I think *Femme* is due for the chop. Your sales figures are hardly brilliant, are they? Perhaps ordinary people have got tired of reading unrealistic articles telling them they ought to be having orgasms twice daily while climbing Mount Everest!'

Normally Shannon would have worried about what office gossip he might have heard. She did briefly wonder, what makes him so sure *I'm* the one who's going to suffer from the downsizing? But her temper had begun to get the better of her.

'So having orgasms is unrealistic, is it?' she purred. 'In that case, I'm sorry for the women you go to bed with!'

'Normal people,' Richard stressed, slurring his words very slightly, 'don't have sex at the drop of a pair of knickers! Your readership, even in this enlightened age, mostly have routine sex in the bedroom with their partners, when they're not too tired after working till nine at the office. People want *fantasy*, like *Babes!*'

'How patronising. I think people want fantasy *and* reality,' Shannon said silkily. 'I always thought

10

Babes! – tacky and naff soft porn though it undoubtedly is – was intended as an *Argos Catalogue* of novel sexual ideas for people to actually put into practice . . . What a shame that you don't have any confidence in your own magazine!'

'Oh my Gawd.' Gary tugged at her arm. 'Time to go to bed, tiger.'

Shannon ignored him. She prodded an unsteady finger across the bar table at Richard Stanley and his superior smile.

'People are a lot more adventurous than you think!'

'Rubbish!' Richard snapped, red-faced. 'At the very best, it's fantasy. That's why people buy these magazines. They never *do* that kind of thing!'

'I do,' Shannon protested. 'I used to be a real mouse. But all I needed was a challenge.'

The fair-haired man leaned back in his seat. He abruptly changed tack. 'Yes, Shannon, but we're talking about normal people. Normal women.' Richard glanced around at the group of men, most of whom were looking back and forth at him and Shannon and grinning. 'You can't call yourself representative. Bit more adventurous than the norm. *Lots* more adventurous, if what I've heard is true!'

'Women having sex is normal!' Shannon felt stung. She eased back in her seat, flexing her stocking-clad feet under the table. Her feet hurt, her head was beginning to feel the effect of too much coffee and too much late-night drinking. The background muzak irritated her almost as much as the way that Richard Stanley raised his eyes to the ceiling and smiled pityingly.

'Shannon, my dear. Other people are so much

11

more tame than you think. Why do you imagine *Femme* is so signally failing to succeed? The average woman doesn't dare do what your articles say she should. And if she does – she doesn't *enjoy* it.'

'Oh, really?' Shannon said. 'Patronising sod. You should never underestimate "ordinary" people. If you'd ever looked under the surface, you'd know *that*. You take any ordinary person – take anyone on your magazine staff, say, or in the *Femme* office. I bet you anything you like, they're already sexually adventurous enough to turn your hair grey!' She paused. 'And anything one of your people would do, one of my people would do double!'

Raucous cheers broke out from the group at the bar. Shannon realised she had got loud. She glanced down and smoothed her satin skirt over her knees.

In a much quieter voice she said, 'How did I get into a dumb argument like that?'

Richard Stanley's smile was rueful. He scratched at his short blond hair, his suit-sleeve pulling up far enough to show the Rolex watch he wore. 'By being dumb, I suppose.'

His tone was friendly – for a moment she didn't register what he had said.

Richard stood. He leaned over the back of her chair. His smile sharpened to malice. She became very conscious of his wide shoulders, and the wiry fair hair on his wrists, and the strong fingers weighed down by gold signet rings. His body was oppressive, looming over her.

'My dear girl,' Richard Stanley said. 'You know very well that *Femme* doesn't stand a chance in any kind of competition with *Babes!*. I picked my staff personally. We're hardly ordinary. If it came down

to it, do you really think the staff of a ladies' magazine could be more raunchy than my people, who
do hard-core fantasy photo shoots? I think not. Get
real.'

You've changed your tune, haven't you . . . Talk
about male ego!

Get stuffed! leapt to Shannon's lips. She
restrained herself. She smiled sweetly. 'Then you
don't have *anything* to worry about at tomorrow's
conference meeting, do you? Mr Howard will pat
you on the back and say "well done". He won't
kick you in the backside, and say "you're redundant!" '

Richard scowled. He could not be much over
thirty, Shannon thought, but when he frowned and
stuck his lower lip out, he looked like a sulkily
unattractive two-year-old. In a suit. The thought
was comic.

'And what are you grinning at?' he snarled, his
poise gone.

'You'll never know . . .' Shannon picked up her
shoes, and padded across the bar to the Ladies' in
her stockinged feet, swinging her hips (even in her
business suit's tight skirt) and smiling with an air
of happiness and slight inebriation.

*And it would have stayed nothing but a bit of 2 a.m.
drunken rubbish*, she thought later – *if only Edmund
Howard hadn't been drinking in the other bar . . .*

She emerged from the Ladies' some minutes
later, pausing at the door to drop her shoes and
wiggle first one and then the other black-
stockinged foot into them. She held on to the
polished wooden door jamb as she did so. The
carpeted floor was showing a distinct inclination
to tilt.

13

'Time for bed,' she sang to herself.

A voice behind her said, 'I wonder if I could have a moment of your time.'

The muggy room settled back on its axis. Someone opened a window somewhere. The cool air of an early summer morning cut through the alcoholic fug. Shannon tucked her curly red-brown hair behind her ears, settled her feet firmly in her high-heeled shoes, straightened her back, and turned to look at the Managing Director of Midnight Rose International.

'Of course, Mr Howard,' she said. Her tongue felt too large and furry for her mouth. Her stomach plummeted. *He wouldn't tell me I'm being made redundant now, would he?*

Edmund Howard stood in the doorway of the private bar. Everything from his dark Savile Row suit to his hand-made leather shoes breathed wealth. At nearly sixty, he was as tall and upright as a much younger man. His hair shone silver. His face was deeply creased.

It was not his clothes that gave him the impact he made on people. It was his eyes. Brilliant blue – and they hit you like a hammer. Edmund Howard was the only man Shannon had ever met who could stand at the far end of a sixty-foot conference hall and you could *still* see that his eyes were blue.

'And Richard.' He did not raise his voice, but Richard Stanley immediately left the group at the bar and walked across the room towards them. Shannon again wondered how Richard managed to look so uncrumpled.

'Here.' Edmund Howard held open the door to the private bar.

It was much quieter here, Shannon realised as

she walked in, preceding Richard. No music, better carpets, deeper armchairs, and the staff behind the bar looked entirely unaware that it was the early hours of the morning.

So did the group of elderly men sitting on leather chairs at the far end of the bar. Edmund Howard acknowledged them with a nod, but did not rejoin them. He seated himself in an armchair by the dark window. 'Now.'

Shannon obeyed his pointing finger and sat down. The deep leather armchair almost swallowed her. She heard Richard give a slight grunt as he sat down opposite her. A waiter brought small glasses of spirits without being asked. Shannon let her brandy remain on the table.

She met the Managing Director's hard gaze. 'I like *Femme*. It took me four years to get to be editor. I don't want to be told the magazine's cancelled. Is that what I'm here for?'

It was a gamble, but in four years of working for the company he ran, she had always found he appreciated honesty, and the blunter the better.

Edmund Howard inclined his head. 'Possibly.'

Shannon felt her stomach go cold.

Richard cleared his throat and muttered, 'Then perhaps I shouldn't be here, sir.'

Edmund Howard leaned his elbows on the arms of the chair and steepled his fingers. His gaze moved from Richard to Shannon, and back again.

'If I were firing people on the grounds of idiocy,' he said, 'then I expect that *both* of you would currently be clearing your desks. I am in the process of talking to my business colleagues here about Midnight Rose International. I do not require two junior editors having a drunken and

15

very loud conversation in the next bar. Do you understand me?'

Shannon Garrett ignored Richard's wince and took her courage in both hands. She smiled at Edmund Howard. 'Drunken, loud, but interesting?' she suggested.

There was a pause. The skin around Howard's blue eyes crinkled. The MD of Midnight Rose International smiled. Shannon noted the slightest suggestion of a sheen on his skin. Edmund Howard was not, she realised, one hundred per cent sober himself.

' "Interesting" is one way of putting it. In fact, it gave rise to a little bet between myself and my colleagues. That need not concern you, except that it has brought me to a decision.' He paused to sip from his glass and savour the fine brandy. He returned his startlingly blue gaze to Shannon. She sat tensely in the deep armchair. She was aware of Richard squirming opposite. Her mouth was dry.

'Sadly,' Edmund Howard went on, 'keeping both *Femme* and *Babes!* on the newsstands is proving uneconomic. You are aware that I have decided to cancel one of the titles. Your sales figures are much the same. In all other respects, there is very little to choose between the magazines – almost nothing, in fact. I need to make a decision by the end of this month. And, overhearing your conversation, I have decided to let it stand on the issue of who wins your contest – who, in my judgement, has the most sexually adventurous person working for their magazine.'

Richard Stanley gave a high-pitched laugh that cut off immediately as he realised the MD was not joining in. Shannon saw his face lose colour. She herself smothered a giggle. She stared at the older man in the armchair.

Edmund Howard regarded them with a quizzical smile. 'I might add, I intend that the person who gains the most – *satisfaction* – from an encounter shall be deemed the winner. Not one who merely consents to perform it.'

'But we didn't – we haven't – there isn't—' Shannon Garrett stopped. She realised her voice had crept up to falsetto. She swallowed and started again. 'Excuse me, sir, but are you quite serious?'

'I don't make jokes.'

The faint undertone of menace made Shannon realise, this is a man who deals in billions, who is ruthless in business, *who can afford the occasional caprice* . . . and I think we're it.

'I'll speak to you both once the conference is over and we're back at home office,' Edmund Howard said briskly. 'Meanwhile, I suggest you think of . . . candidates.' His lined face became cold as he watched his two seated employees. 'Unless you'd prefer me to make up my mind now, on the flip of a coin? That might be more sensible.'

Shannon was about to say *yes, forget the whole idea, this whole thing is completely untenable!*

And then, out of the corner of her eye, she saw Richard Stanley grin.

It was more of a smirk. The blond man, in his executive's suit and his expensive male jewellery, leaned back in the armchair and crossed his leg over his knee. His grin was aimed at her. It said, very plainly, *you don't dare.*

'You want to bet?' Shannon murmured under her breath. She looked back at the Managing Director and gave him a dazzling smile. 'I think it's a wonderfully *creative* solution, sir. I have no objection, if Richard hasn't.'

It's economics, she thought, as she enjoyed Richard's weak attempt to smile. One of the titles is going to go. His or mine. We could let it be decided by some anonymous suit down in Accounts. Or we can do this.

I want to do this!

'It's rather unfair on Shannon,' Richard recovered. 'But I agree with you, sir, it's a good way of settling this. To the end of this month?'

'Yes.' The silver-haired man stood up from the armchair. The only sign of his age was the way that he momentarily took his weight on his wrists as he gripped the chair-arms and pushed himself up.

'My secretary will deliver the bets,' Edmund Howard said.

'Bets?' Her rival editor unconsciously wiped at his upper lip. Richard said, 'How do you mean, sir, "bets"?'

Shannon managed to stand up without falling back into the deep burgundy armchair. She beamed with inebriated satisfaction. 'I said all anyone needed to be sexually adventurous was a challenge. You said any one of *Femme*'s staff didn't stand a chance against any one of the staff of *Babes!*. I think Mr Howard is going to suggest the challenges. The bets. The things we bet our staff will do – will *enjoy* regarding as a challenge! And if they don't enjoy the experience . . . they lose!'

'Exactly.' Edmund Howard's grip under her elbow was strong and steadying. Shannon had not realised she was swaying. 'Good night.'

'Good night, sir.' Richard stood.

Shannon concentrated on not falling off her

heels. Once through the closed doors of the hotel's private bar, she leaned back against them and let out a long breath.

'I don't believe it!' she exclaimed. 'He's nuts!'

'He's the MD,' Richard Stanley said soberly. His bloodshot eyes were dazed. 'He can be nuts. He can do this sort of thing any time he likes.'

'It's . . . the fourteenth today? That only gives us a fortnight! This is going to be . . .' Shannon gave an amazed chuckle '. . . fun! Unbelievable, ridiculous, but fun!'

The other bar was empty. Even Gary had gone up to his room. She picked up her jacket from the back of her chair. A warm, sweaty male hand touched her back. It felt wet through her silk shirt.

Richard's hand slid down over her skirt and caressed her bottom. His brandy-smelling breath brushed her cheek. 'No reason why we shouldn't start at the top, Shannon. Let's say we see what *Femme*'s editor is willing to do. How adventurous will you be? Huh?'

Shannon moved her elbow sharply back as she turned to face him. He grunted and fell back a step.

Shannon said sweetly, 'Just because I'm uninhibited, that doesn't mean I'm not choosy!'

His expression was wonderful to see. Shannon giggled. 'Good night, Richard,' she smiled.

She reached the bottom of the stairs. He called after her, in a malicious whisper, 'Don't *forget*, Shannon. When all the girls in your office tell you that you're crazy, and that they're never going to do anything like that, and it's the end of this month, and your crummy little mag ends up down the toilet – *don't forget that you agreed to this!*'

*

Shannon Garrett fell back across the hotel bed, the following morning's headache throbbing and stabbing behind her eyes.

'He's right. I agreed.' She threw her arm across her face to block out the dawn sunlight. She forgot the rest of the conference and thought ahead to Monday.

Monday, back in the office. With the editorial staff.

Shannon chuckled. 'They're not going to tell me I'm crazy. In fact, I think I'm going to be knocked down in the rush!'

Chapter Three

'YOU'RE CRAZY! I'M never going to do anything like that!'

'But I *have* to find someone!' Shannon wailed. 'Come on, Julia, you're not going to let me down. Are you?'

Julia Royston, the redheaded deputy editor of *Femme*, looked at her askance. 'Now tell me this is a joke. Okay? Tell me this is your sense of humour. *Please?*'

Shannon cupped her hands around a mug bearing the legend *Give Me The Coffee And No One Gets Hurt*. She took a deep breath and smiled at the older woman. 'Oh – of course it is! You know what the conference is like. Adrenaline panic. I just thought you'd like to hear the depths to which late-night bar-talk can descend!'

Julia, whose fortysomething calm had begun to seem curled at the edges, relaxed and smiled. 'You do have a way of getting me going, Shannon. Now. About this article on lingerie; it's late in . . .'

The back of the office chair dug into Shannon's shoulder-blades. She wriggled. The smart blue cotton summer dress she had bought on the way back from the convention was already marked with sweat under the arms. The *Femme* office's air-conditioning couldn't cope with the heatwave.

Damn! That's everybody. All my staff. I've raised the subject with them all. They *all* think it's a joke – or want to think it is. And today's the eighteenth. *Now* what?

She sipped the acrid coffee and tried to get her mind back on to the October issue of the magazine.

Her gaze strayed over her workstation monitor and out of her tiny, paper-filled office. A slim young woman with silver-blonde hair was emerging, rump-first, from under a desk. She dusted the knees of a pair of raw silk harem-pants with casual efficiency.

'Her,' Shannon interrupted Julia, ignoring her deputy editor's sigh. 'The girl with her bum under David's desk – I've forgotten her name.'

'Alix something.' Julia's copper-coloured eyebrows lifted. 'Alix Neville. She's on a contract to come and sort out our IT equipment every three months. Last time she set our local network up.'

'That's right. I remember talking to her way back in January . . .' Shannon drained her coffee mug. 'Take the lingerie article out and put the winter fashion article in. Drop the sexual compatibility quiz. Tell Sandra it would be really good if we could have the piece on sex with best friends' exes for October instead of November. And hold my calls, I'm taking an early lunch.'

On her way out of the office, Shannon stopped by the desk at which the silver-blonde woman was working.

'Alix, isn't it? Fancy lunch?'

The young woman looked up, presenting

Shannon with a pair of grey eyes as clear as cold water. She nodded once.

'Let's order.' Shannon handed the menu back to the waiter, asked for salad. Fierce sunlight on the London pavements was muted here, through the bistro's darkened windows. Fragments of light glinted from glasses, knives, and Alix Neville's amazing hair. She was an inch or two taller than Shannon's five foot five. Her slight build, and the long silver-blonde hair caught up over her ears, gave her an elfin look. Her face was wide at the temples, sharp at the chin.

Alix's gathered harem-pants and silk tank-top clung to a smooth-hipped and small-breasted figure. A stray curling tendril of hair lay across the ecru silk at her shoulder and the skin at the base of her throat. Her skin gleamed. There was a hint of muscle that made Shannon think the younger woman worked out in a gym, and that her slight build might be deceptive.

Alix Neville smiled unexpectedly. She had a gamine grin. 'So why am I having lunch with the boss? And why is the boss looking at me as if I were prize bloodstock?'

Heat rose to Shannon's cheeks. 'Was I? Sorry.'

A twinkle appeared in the younger woman's eye. 'I thought perhaps I was supposed to blush, and say "this is so sudden".'

Shannon Garrett's head went back and she whooped with laughter. Conversation stopped for a second across the room. Someone dropped a fork. She muffled her mouth with her hand.

Alix said evenly, 'Do I get to find out what's going on?'

Shannon reached across and squeezed the young woman's arm briefly. 'Yes. Sorry. I really do have to tell you what all this is about. You are one of my staff, after all, even if it is on contract. And you'll tell me to get lost, but, hey,' Shannon smiled ruefully, 'that'll make the ninth one this morning. You have absolutely no reason at all to be interested in my problems.'

The young woman shook her head and grinned. 'You're going to tell me anyway. What is this all about?'

Shannon thought, I could like this girl.

'Well.' Shannon took a deep breath. 'It's like this.'

She watched the younger woman's face as she explained. Alix's expression became still, and then gradually a smile flicked up one corner of her mouth. She leaned her elbows on the table and covered her lips with her short-nailed fingers. Her grey eyes began to sparkle. She stared at Shannon for some minutes after Shannon stopped speaking.

'Well, now.' Alix dropped her hands palm-down on the polished wooden table. 'Oh, wow! Well . . .'

Shannon said hastily, 'Since you work on contract, you're not in the office all the time. You wouldn't suffer from office gossip. But you do work for *Femme*. You're ideal!'

'So I've been told,' the girl said dryly. She flicked a gaze up at Shannon from under dark eyebrows. 'Usually it's been for my technological skills.'

Shannon glanced through the window, across the Japanese bikes parked at the kerb, to the jugglers and Chinese dancers on the cobbled concourse opposite. The bistro occupied a corner site across from Covent Garden. A faint sound of

24

bells chimed over the conversations of the other diners. Women in bright linen dresses, men in shirt-sleeves, electronic diaries open between them on the tables, sparkling cutlery . . .

Shannon eased back on her chair. Sweat tacked the blue cotton dress to the swell of her breasts and hips. Her bare legs and feet in her sandals were grimy from dust picked up on the short walk from the taxi. She sipped her fizzy water, then picked out her lemon slice and sucked it dry.

'Don't feel obliged,' Shannon muttered hastily. 'I mean, there's no pressure, of course you don't have to do this. I don't suppose losing one contract matters that much to you, if *Femme* gets cancelled. I mean – well, what I mean is – oh, damn! What are you laughing at?'

The younger woman swivelled round in her chair so that she could stretch out her legs. Long legs, in oatmeal-coloured loose silk gathered at the ankle. Shannon's gaze moved up the sweep of Alix's body – neatly sandalled feet, slim ankles, the hinted-at curves of calf and thigh; her flat belly under her tank-top, and the swell of her breasts under heat-dampened silk. Alix held her head with a certain poise, looking at Shannon from under dark lashes. From what Shannon could see of her roots, her startling white-blonde hair colour was completely natural.

'Me? Laughing?' Alix said. 'Because I don't even know – look, Ms Garrett, can I at least call you by your first name? Given the subject we're discussing!'

'It's Shannon,' Shannon said. 'Oh, good grief. I'm not very good at this, am I?'

Shannon sat back as the waiter appeared with

their orders. She prodded the devoured lemon slice around the surface of the table, and then prodded salad unenthusiastically around her plate with her fork. Alix Neville shovelled king prawns into her mouth as if she hadn't eaten for a week.

'No breakfast,' Alix explained through a mouthful of food.

Shannon nodded morosely. The younger woman had a mobile mouth, with a full lower lip from which she now wiped sauce with a finger. Shannon watched her suck her finger clean, skin glistening.

'Richard is right. I was wrong about people. It was a stupid idea. Forget I mentioned it.' Shannon stood up.

'Wait!' The young women dropped a prawn, her fork and her napkin, reaching up to grab Shannon's arm. Her fingers were sticky again with sauce. 'Look, don't go! Not yet. Let's talk about this! I didn't say I *didn't* want to!'

Shannon looked down into the gamine face. 'I was just going to the Ladies', actually.'

'Oh.' Alix took her hand away. A pink flush coloured her fine-textured skin from her cheeks down to her collarbone.

'I'll be back in a minute,' Shannon said.

In the restaurant's powder room, she washed the sauce fingerprints from her arm. Even the cold tap ran with warm water. She dipped her face into cupped hands full of water and stood up. The drops runnelled down her neck, under the bodice of her cotton dress, dampening the cloth and her breasts and simultaneously drying from her body-heat.

The room door opened. Alix Neville entered.

'You're not kidding me, are you?' The younger woman stepped up to the wash-basins and ran the cold tap. She put her wrists under it in a vain attempt to cool down.

They stood beside each other. Her eyes met Shannon's eyes in the mirror.

'I mean, if I say *yes*, does Jeremy Beadle leap out with a camera team?'

'I sincerely hope not,' Shannon muttered.

'Because, if this is genuine . . .'

'Yes. It is. If you ever meet Edmund Howard – the big boss – you'll know exactly why.' Shannon inhaled the muggy air. 'He has a whim of case-hardened steel. This actually *is* the way he's going to decide whether *Femme* sinks or swims.'

Alix grinned at her in the mirror. 'Never mind the magazine. I've met Richard Stanley – I want to make that pig eat his words!'

Shannon felt her mouth move irresistibly into an answering smile. 'Now you come to mention it – so do I!'

Alix's eyes sparkled. She turned away from the mirror. 'Then phone me the minute the bet comes through. Today. Tonight! Any time. I can't wait to get started on this! But, Shannon, there is one more thing.'

'What's that?' Shannon leaned forward, slicking a light lipstick onto her lower lip.

In the mirror, she saw Alix Neville move closer. The young woman reached out a small, strong hand. She slid it around Shannon's waist, up the dampened material of her dress, until her palm pressed against the full roundness of Shannon's breast. A sudden unexpected warmth flowered in Shannon's groin. Her breath caught in her throat.

'If one of the bets is about women,' Alix Neville said, 'I'll come and talk to my boss. Okay?'

Shannon's mobile phone shrilled from her bag. She grabbed at it. Speaking, she still kept her gaze on Alix. 'What? Yes. About finished . . . *What?* Okay. No, it's a message for me. A personal message. Don't worry about it. I'll be back in two minutes!'

She flipped the phone shut.

'That was Julia. A messenger just came down from the penthouse office.' Shannon looked at the younger woman, suddenly breathless. 'With an envelope from the MD. This is it! We're off. You're sure you don't want to change your mind?'

Alix Neville slid her palm over her own breast, down her stomach to her thighs. 'Shannon, I'm so turned on now, I can't think about anything else! No, I do *not* want to change my mind. Let's get going!'

Femme's twentieth-floor offices looked down over workaday London from Canary Wharf. Office-block windows shimmered in the August heat. Light twinkled up from chrome fenders and from wing-mirrors. Shannon opened her cubicle-office window the two inches that it *would* open. Faint engine sounds drifted up. The urgent conversations of her staff getting the magazine under way cut off as Alix shut the office door behind them.

'Okay. Let's look.' Shannon lifted the plain cream envelope.

A tiny clear space in the cubicle had a visitor's chair in it. Alix Neville did not sit down. She stood on the one remaining piece of floor not covered with files, boxes and back copies of *Femme*. Her sandalled feet were in a patch of sunlight. She looked up and met Shannon's gaze. Her eyes were wide and dark, her pupils dilated to velvet-black holes.

'It feels like the top of a ski-slope,' she confessed. 'The point of no return. Knowing that I'm going to push myself into it, any second, and then – wheee!'

The thin cotton material of her bra and panties became taut over Shannon's flesh at the thought. Arousal swelled her breasts. She tried to force it out of her mind.

'Okay . . .' Shannon slid the pad of her finger along the top of the envelope. The paper rasped against her skin. Abruptly she slid her finger under the flap and ripped it open. She took out a page of heavy cream vellum.

The writing was old-fashioned fountain-pen script.

Shannon began to read aloud.

Chapter Four

I NEED THIS, Alix Neville suddenly realised. I don't just *want* to do it. I *need* to do it.

She slid her two-year-old silver Audi neatly into a parking space. The immense car park around the out-of-London shopping mall was almost full. Young couples walked past. A small child ran, and was picked up by its mother. As she opened the car door, she heard the growl of engines and the shouts of distant youths. The mall building's glass roof glittered like Kew Gardens' greenhouses.

Alix slid her legs around and got out of her car. Her sheer stockings hissed together. Her full-skirted lacy white summer dress tangled around her thighs. She stooped to tug it free. The cotton bodice momentarily pulled tight across her small, full breasts. The day smelled of late, late summer; when the heat is old but has not outstayed its welcome.

And why do I need this? Because I was bored. *Am* bored. Bored, and I didn't know it!'

Alix Neville, twenty-four, ice-blonde, exotic – well, English with a French grandmother – and a highly qualified freelance computer consultant, she thought to herself. Sounds good, doesn't it?

She picked her mobile phone up off the seat and put it into her shoulder-bag. She put on RayBans, giving the hot afternoon a sepia tone.

I have to admit, I'm extremely well paid for what I do. It's a job with high prestige, especially in a man's world. *And I'm bored to tears.* I work, I go out, I meet a guy, he doesn't like it that I earn more than he does, he doesn't like it that I can come more often than he does, he doesn't like it that I'm smarter than he is, and where does that leave me? Bored to tears with dickless wonders.

Well, okay. Maybe they're cute. But I am what I am.

So let's have some no-nonsense, no-strings, good old-fashioned *lust.* Just for once, it's *my* turn.

'Hello?' She stabbed the buttons on the mobile phone. 'Hello, Simon. There you are. I was beginning to think you'd got lost. No, I'll meet you inside. No. No! You'll find out.' Alix chuckled. 'Trust me!'

She began to walk across the car park towards the six-storey shopping mall. Sunlight fractured off the myriad glass windows of the cupola. Gulls wheeled above, shrieking. She licked dry lips. It seemed an age and no time at all until she stood outside the big glass and chrome doors.

'Watch it!' A man wearing a sports shirt and medallion pushed past her.

Alix shook off her absent-mindedness. She stepped through the doors, into the air-conditioned coolness of the mall. Noise hit her. A thousand voices, men and women and children, talking and shouting and shrieking. The sunlight through the glass of the central cupola fell on their bright clothes. Like being in an aviary, she realised. She walked on, the high heels of her sandals clicking on the polished floor.

If I knew what Shannon's boss Mr Howard looked like, I could try to spot him. Will he be here himself? Will he watch? Or just have someone else watching, to report back to him?

Alix shook her head ruefully. The long curls of her silver-white hair fell about her bare shoulders. She had caught her hair up with side combs, and she wore gold studs in her ears. Tall, elegant – she knew the picture she must make.

'Alix?' a male voice said.

Alix walked up to the rail that surrounded the central atrium. A man leaned on the barrier, beside the glass-fronted lifts that rose and fell: six storeys up, six stories down. She said, 'Simon.'

The man's gaze dropped to take in the swell of her breasts under the white dress, the nipped-in waist, and the flare of the full skirt over her narrow hips. Alix leaned her elbows on the rail beside him.

Simon was in his early thirties; tall, and broad across the shoulders. His light brown hair was cropped very short. It was intended to be tidy, but little tufts still stuck up at the back. He regarded Alix with a blank expression.

I never could read him, Alix thought. Perhaps that's the attraction.

'Cheer up, Simon,' she said. 'We're going shopping.'

'You phoned me in my lunch hour to come out here to go *shopping* with you? Wouldn't one of your girlfriends have been better?' His voice was light for such a big man, and resonant.

'You don't know me well enough to know what my girlfriends are like,' Alix pointed out. She scooched over on the rail until her thigh rested against his. His pale blue jeans were worn soft as moleskin. The small solidity of her garter strap, under her dress, pressed against him through the double layer of cloth. 'And I don't think you know much about shopping.'

'I—' He coughed. He glanced swiftly at her, and then stared out over the central atrium. 'Yes. Right. Er . . '

Alix leaned beside him and gazed down into the well, down at the heads of the people below. An ever-moving crowd. She watched faces. Eyes that did not stray from their own concerns.

'Come on.' She raised her eyes to his, pressing her thigh closer. Simon's breath hitched. His chest rose and fell in the white T-shirt that fitted him tightly. His eyes focused on her, as if he saw her for the first time.

'That's better. I got sick of going to your offices, and you not noticing me.'

His voice was thick when he finally spoke. 'I'm noticing you now.'

'So I see.' Alix's lashes dipped as she glanced down. There was a perceptible bulge in his jeans.

'Sorry,' he said. 'Or am I?'

Alix smiled wickedly. 'I hope not.'

That seemed to relax something in him. He laughed, his eyes bright, and dropped one arm around her waist. The reflected sunlight gleamed on the fine black hairs of his forearm. His skin felt hot against the material of her dress.

She rested her hand briefly on his before slipping out of his embrace. 'Not so fast, tiger.

33

Shopping was what I said, and shopping was what I meant . . . first.'

'Alix—' He frowned.

'This way!' She took his hand. His strong fingers grasped hers, tightening after a moment. Alix weaved her way expertly between the thronging people, hips swinging, Simon struggling to keep up. 'There!'

Without waiting for his reply, Alix drifted into the lingerie shop. The assistant eyed her, bored, and then looked away. Alix slid the tips of her fingers across a silk teddy and glanced up at the man beside her.

'Like it?' she said. 'Feel it.'

His hand left hers. Obediently, he stroked the cool fabric. His expression was quietly intent. And far too controlled.

Alix put her hand down by her side. Hidden by the folds of her skirt, she slid her palm onto his thigh, and upwards. The muscle of his leg twitched under her hand. Deliberately, she moved her hand up to his crotch. She put her fingers between his legs and cupped the bulge in his pants in her moist palm. His cock leapt under her touch. When she looked up, he was staring at the shop wall and the display of silk knickers. Light sweat beaded his forehead.

'Like it?'

'Good God, woman! We're in public. We're in a shopping mall!'

That sent her off into giggles. Both her hands went over her mouth. The shop assistant glared. Alix turned, brushing her hip against Simon's hip again, and swayed out of the store, her walk deliberately provocative.

'Well,' she murmured, her voice still shaking with laughter, 'you can't have me in private. But you can have me in public.'

He walked out of the shop awkwardly. She noticed he now held his light summer jacket folded over his arms in front of him so that the material hid him from waist to knee.

'*What* did you say?' Simon blurted.

'Once-in-a-lifetime offer, never to be repeated,' Alix chuckled. 'I want to fuck you, Simon. I'm going to fuck you. And I'm going to fuck you here, now, with everybody watching.' She let him sweat for a second before she added, 'Except no one's going to notice what we're doing.'

'What?' Simon's brown eyes were animated now. He scratched at his ear, looked away, looked back, and then laughed. 'Woman, you're crazy.'

Alix smoothed her hands over the folds of her full cotton skirt. 'I'm not wearing any knickers under this.'

His breath caught in his throat. Their eyes locked.

Alix's smile faded. In a thick voice, she said, 'Now.'

He nodded his cropped head once. He reached out and put his hands around her waist. His hands felt strong, warm – then hot. His grip tightened on her until she gasped. Slowly he brought her forward until she was pressed against him. Her breasts pushed against his firm chest, her belly against his flat stomach and the solid hardness of his erect cock. Warmth flowered in her groin. She pressed her thighs against his, only a thin layer of material separating her skin from his, her smooth flesh from his hairy roughness.

35

'God damn you, Alix!' Simon growled. 'You can't do this to a man.'

'Just *watch* what I can do to a man,' Alix said huskily. 'And in full view, too . . .'

Slowly, deliberately, she turned around in his embrace. His hands still gripped her, but now they rested on the smooth cotton front of her bodice. His hips and cock jutted against the smooth swell of her buttocks, under her full, concealing cotton skirt. His embrace tightened, making it hard for her to breathe.

Alix rested her forearms on the varnished wooden rail. She braced her feet in her high-heeled sandals slightly apart. Looking out over the atrium, she said, very quietly and very intensely, 'Fuck me.'

Sunlight slanted down through the glass cupola and made the empty air glow. The shops on the floors the other side of the mall blurred in her vision. Heat and sweat rolled from her shoulders, down her breasts, and under the neck of the thin dress.

He choked. 'You don't know. I've thought about this. Often. I *want*—'

Alix felt herself pressed hard up against the rail. Its metal struts pressed against the front of her thighs. Simon's large, hard body jammed up against her, the sheer strength of him exhilarating.

She felt the smooth denim of his jeans snag on her dress. His erect cock rubbed at the cleft between her buttocks. *Thank God I wore wore heels . . .*

She felt him gradually, carefully, pull up the back of her summer dress. The wide folds of it fell down, swathing her legs and concealing his thighs and hips.

His hot hand caressed the swell of her buttocks.

Her pussy grew instantly wet. Involuntarily she thrust back against him. He groaned in her ear.

'Oh, look,' Alix mimed. She pointed, as if she were innocently leaning on the rail to point out something in the view of shops and thronging crowds that was of interest. She pushed her cool buttocks back into his hot hand. He made a noise in the back of his throat.

His body remained perfectly still. His hand slipped between her thighs. One thick, stubby, short-nailed finger probed up into her hot wetness. She slid down a fraction of an inch, bringing it between her outer labia. The lips of her sex throbbed hotly. His hand dripped with her juices.

'Oh yes . . .' Simon's voice growled centimetres behind her ear. She couldn't see his face, his brown eyes, his stolid expression. His hard, thick finger slid in and out of her, slowly, teasing. She braced her legs apart.

Alix put her hand behind her. She felt his cock leap in his pants. Slowly she took the zip of his jeans between finger and thumb and tugged. The size of his erect penis was too large for her to drag the zip down.

'Let's make this exciting.' She slid sideways along the rail, out of the man's embrace.

'*What?*'

'Not far,' Alix said thickly. 'Don't you know, anticipation is half of pleasure?'

'*No!*'

Half a dozen people turned round to stare at them. Simon did not look stolid now. His cheeks were flushed, his eyes bright, and his pupils dark and dilated. He clenched his fists. Muscles bulged on his forearms, biceps and shoulders under his white T-shirt. Standing this close, she could smell sex-sweat on him, tangy and rough and musky.

She didn't speak. She flirted her silver-blonde eyebrows at him and walked away. She almost stumbled, unsteady on her heels.

My God, my legs are like water! He'd *better* follow me. I'm not going to be left like this!

She risked a glance over her shoulder.

The big man was following her, his jacket clutched grimly in front of his crotch.

Alix walked unsteadily to the lifts that serviced the six floors of the shopping centre. Voices rang in her ears, half-sentences of conversations caught as she walked by, a screaming baby, a woman's throaty, chuckling laugh. You and me too, babe, she thought. Her pussy was deliciously hot and wet. It ached for satisfaction. It ached for fullness. Her palm remembered the thick girth of his erect cock.

I want him inside me! I want him *now*!

The lift doors parted in front of her with a soft sigh. Light sparkled. The lifts were glass-fronted. Brass-coloured fittings held glass cages that slid up and down the walls of the central atrium.

Alix stepped in. Two or three other people followed. Simon stepped in after her and sidled his way across the narrow lift.

Alix gazed out at the well of the building and at the other lifts. She ignored a conversation that a woman in the lift was having with her boyfriend. She was conscious only of Simon as he eased in beside her.

Alix turned so that she faced out over the atrium. She looked out through the glass. A brass rail ran around the inside of the lift, at hip-height. She reached down and closed her hands around the slick metal bar.

Simon moved his body against hers. He looked across her shoulder, out across the mall. Neon lights and bright plastic store fronts glittered. The lift smelled of close, hot, summer humanity. The conversations, and the hiss of the lift doors opening and shutting, passed though her consciousness all but unnoticed.

Quiet, a mere breath, she murmured, 'Fuck me now.'

There was no way for him to remonstrate. He can't argue, she thought, with people in the lift who can hear us.

A quick glance at the reflection in the lift's glass wall assured her that the six other people in the lift were travelling facing the inside wall, watching the doors and the floor indicators. The reflection in the glass wall also showed her her own face, flushed, among tumbling silver-white curls. And Simon, his eyes hooded, his lips slightly parted. His breath feathered her ear.

No way to argue, she thought. Okay, boy. You either do it or you don't.

Her breathing quickened. She felt her breasts swell with arousal, nipples pressing at the fabric of her summer dress. The cotton stretched. A faint pink flush coloured her skin.

In the reflection, his shoulders moved.

With agonising slowness, she felt the back of her dress pulled up. No one in the lift gave her a second glance. The folds of material fell around his hips and crotch at the sides. At the front, her skirt fell straight down, hiding her from the open well of the atrium, and the crowds on the mall floor opposite. She felt the hem of the back of her skirt pushed up over the swell of her buttocks.

Sweat and juices slicked the insides of her cool thighs.

In the glass wall of the lift, she watched one of Simon's hands vanish into the folds of material at his side. She felt his knuckles press against the smooth, bare skin of her thigh.

His fingers touched the lacy tops of her sheer stockings. She felt the pressure dimple her skin. Suddenly his hand gripped hard. She almost gasped aloud. His hand went up her stocking, to her garter strap, to the bare fold of flesh between the back of her thigh and her bottom. His thumb probed towards her pussy.

She froze. Her back wanted to arch. She held herself rigidly still.

His hot, hard hand slipped back to cup her hip. His breath thickened. His hand moved forward over her hips, down to the curve of her belly. Nothing showed outside her skirts. The sensitive skin of her stomach twitched, and she had to bite her lip to stop a reaction.

His short-nailed fingers drove down into the curls of her silver-gold hair. Sweat slicked his fingertips. Her sex ached for him. She thrust her clitoris forward a fraction, meeting his fingers. Slowly, deliciously, he began to touch her. His fingertips feathered across her clit. She leaked juices. She felt her labia swell, engorged. She could not say a word.

The lift halted. The doors hissed. People got out, more people got in. Doors shut. The lift moved up again.

Alix felt Simon's other hand move under her skirts. No one looked. Behind her, a rather loud conversation went on between two young men. Simon's other hand moved under her skirts, towards his crotch. She felt him grip the zip of his jeans and jerk it down.

The hot flesh of his belly slicked against her bottom. Released, the solid tip of his cock pressed urgently against the cleft of her buttocks. Pressing back against him, she felt his breathing stifled and ragged.

She eased up on her heels. Her weight came forward, resting on her hands where she gripped the rail. Her pussy throbbed. As if she were merely shifting her weight, she moved her legs slightly apart.

The head of his glans pushed at her inner lips. Her swollen flesh throbbed. Fraction by fraction, centimetre by centimetre, entirely unhurried, Simon slid his hot hard cock up into her. She rose to the pushing-apart of her flesh, and then sank down on his thick hardness. The bushy hair at his groin rubbed against her inflamed wetness. His balls banged against her bum.

Ooohh yes . . . She swallowed. No one looked at her. The glass cubicle of the lift rose towards the mall roof. Sunlight and a blue summer sky blazed through the glass. His hips came up, and her heels left the heels of her sandals. She stood on tiptoe, hands gripping the lift rail tightly, supported on the iron-hard fullness of his cock.

Slowly, without a word being spoken, he began to thrust up into her.

Alix felt every ridge and vein of his bulging cock as it plunged up into her swollen pussy. Tingles of

41

delight ran across her skin. The little hairs feathering the nape of her neck stood up. Her eyes went wide. His cock moved down, moved up, thrusting her so slowly full of his hardness.

She caught a tiny piece of her lip between her teeth and nipped at her flesh. Her moan did not escape her throat.

His chest rose and fell, pressed against her back. In the glass she could see this floor of the mall reflected as a lift full of people got out – and half a dozen other people got in. The doors hissed shut.

The floor of the lift pushed at her toes. Simon's cock withdrew until the bulge at the head just rested within her outer labia, teasing her. Her sex ached.

This time the lift started with a jerk. The jerk thrust Simon's cock suddenly up her.

It pushed against the faint resistance of her flesh and popped in. And up. And up! Her eyes flew wide. She saw her surprised reflection in the glass, her mouth a startled O. 'Mmmph!'

A woman in a heavy coat gave her an absent-minded look and then went back to talking to her friend.

I have got to come. I can't help it! I'm going to come! Oh God!

Alix bit the inside of her lip. Simon's eyes behind her were half closed. They looked like girlfriend and boyfriend, doing nothing more than leaning against the rail of the lift, sleepy-eyed in the hot summer afternoon.

Oh Jesus, Alix thought. Her sex tightened, then loosened. Impaled, she stretched up as tall as she could on her toes without escaping from his rigid prick. She squeezed his cock inside her. His hands clamped tight on her hips.

He began imperceptibly to thrust.

Oh, shit. Oh, *sheee-it* . . .

It's up to him whether I come or not, Alix realised. Her hands tightened on the metal rail. Her knuckles whitened. There isn't a thing I can do about it. Oh God, I'm so wet. I'm going to make a noise! I *know* I am!

A small baby in a push-chair looked up at her and gurgled as its mother wheeled it backwards out of the lift. Two more men got in. The lift jerked to a start. Alix whimpered. The two men were talking so loudly – about cars – that she went unheard.

'Do it to me,' she whispered, her lips hardly moving. 'Do it to me now!'

The lift ascended towards the fifth floor. His hands on her hips pressed her garter belt deeply into her flesh. His palms ran with sweat.

He thrust. She felt the muscles of her thighs begin to shake. He was a hot velvet hardness inside her slick wet hole. He pumped his cock up into her. The lift was full of talk.

I can hold it. I swear I can hold on . . . *oh!*

Simon's right hand pushed forward, down her hip, over her warm belly. His long blunt middle finger found her clit. Slowly, tantalisingly, he began to rotate the pad of his finger. Sparkles of pleasure shot out from her. She felt her pulse break step. Her breathing quickened. 'Uh . . . *uhhn* . . .'

Delirious, at the point of no return, Alix realised, *I am going to come in front of all these people!*

His finger tormented her clit. His cock thrust up into her sex. Her knees weakened. She held herself up by willpower. Her breath caught in her dry mouth.

The lift doors hissed open. The lift emptied. The lift doors slid shut. The glass cubicle started off up towards the sixth and final floor. And, as the lift cable tightened, it started with a jerk.

'Oh God!' His thick flesh jammed her open. Her knees flexed. Alix's head fell back against his chest. She had one glimpse in the glass's reflection to realise that their lift was empty now.

Across the atrium, sixty feet away, other lifts glided up and down, full of shoppers gazing idly out. The rails of the various floors of the mall were crowded with people leaning and talking, looking out into the void.

A voice in her ear said, 'Now I'm going to make you come.'

The hand that had so expertly manipulated her clit slid up her body. It grabbed her right breast, under her dress, squeezing hard.

Someone will see! she thought. And then couldn't think at all.

His hard fingers gripped her breast, clamping around her almost painfully. Her nipple hardened instantly. With his other hand, he dug his fingers into her hip, under her skirt, almost bodily holding her up. The hair at his groin rasped across her buttocks.

He drew his cock back slowly. 'Take *this*!'

Inexorably, smoothly, unstoppably, he drove his flesh up into hers. His cock felt hot inside her. Fluid slicked her inner thighs. Her mouth fell open. She arched her back, thrusting her body to meet his, slamming down on his prick.

'Oh Jesus!' he exclaimed in a strangulated high moan.

His loss of control undid her. An explosion of

44

pleasure flooded her, taking her completely by surprise. Her sweaty palms slipped off the guard rail. Her eyes flew open. Pleasure soared, peaked, soared again, and she came, thunderously, as he spent his cum into her.

The lift glided to a halt at the sixth floor.

Alix, in a daze, heard the lift doors open and shut. No one got in. The lift started down again. His hot cum began to dribble out of her, coursing down her thighs. He leaned against her, sobbing for breath.

The lift stopped at the fifth floor. A couple got on, and got off at the fourth. Neither of them appeared to notice Alix's rising bosom, or the roughness of her breath as she relaxed back against Simon's strong, hot body.

'Um.' His voice started at a squeak. He got it under control. 'Uh, Alix . . .'

She let her gaze roam the well of the mall as the various floors rose up to meet them. No one that she could see was staring at their lift. No one noticed. No one.

The flesh between her legs throbbed. His dwindling prick slipped out of her.

'Alix, I . . .' His voice trailed off. He met her gaze, in the reflection in the glass. 'Will we – I mean, will you – is this going to happen again?'

'I said this was a once-only offer.' Alix smiled, taking the sting out of it.

The sun shone down into the vast mall. She smoothed her bright hair back from her bare shoulders. Its ends were dark silver with moisture. She turned her head, glancing up over her shoulder.

One hand went behind her back, groping for his groin.

'But lunch hour isn't over yet, Simon.' Alix said.
'Take me to the top floor again . . .'

Chapter Five

THE PHONE GOT Shannon Garrett out of the bath.

It was early in the hot summer evening. She had the bathroom window open, with the scent of lime trees drifting in from the gardens at the back of the west London terrace houses. She rose out of the herbal steam into cool air and dabbed at herself with a soft towel. The big mirror in its mahogany frame showed her glimpses of pink shoulders and calves through condensation.

Her mobile phone was, of course, in the bedroom. She padded through, barefoot.

'Yes – Oh, sorry, Alix. No, my fault, I forgot to take it into the bath with me. Come on, tell me! How did it go?' Shannon listened to the excited voice. A huge grin broke out on her face. 'You didn't! You did. *Great*. Alix, you're a gem. A bloody diamond!'

The younger woman's voice came clearly through. 'Hey, well . . . I really had to grit my teeth for this one.'

'Oh. If you don't like this, Alix, *please* don't do it—'

A peal of laughter echoed down the mobile phone. 'Shannon, I'm *kidding*! I've had my eye on Simon for ages. He's always been so stand-offish. I really hate it when a man looks at me like I'm part of the wallpaper. He won't make *that* mistake again.'

Alix's chuckle was warm and sleepy. Shannon could almost feel her glow of contentment over the phone. 'If I'm not being indelicate, how many times did you . . . succeed, if I can put it that way?'

'Three.' Alix's voice was smug. 'And we weren't spotted! I had a nasty moment when someone brought a dog into the lift and it barked at me! Simon's gone home exhausted. I'm not sure if he's afraid I won't call him again, or afraid that I will!' Her chuckle bubbled down the line. 'So, you'll handle the office end of things?'

Shannon nodded, forgetting she couldn't be seen over the phone. She said, 'Yes. Actually, I only came home for a break and a bath – I'm going back in this evening. I'll probably work till around midnight. I guess I'm going to hear something from upstairs tonight.'

As it turned out, there was a production problem that kept Shannon busy until well after eleven.

'That ought to do it,' she finally announced. 'Okay, take five.'

Julia Royston and a young copy editor left her office, chatting. Shannon leaned back in her chair and exhaled softly. Outside the office windows, the last tinge of sunset had vanished from the London skies. Brilliant twin specks of light moved regularly overhead, sometimes low enough for

Shannon to see their red and green wing lights. The stack of jets circling in from the east to land at Heathrow was hypnotic.

'Ms Garrett.' A young messenger boy knocked apologetically on her open office door. He had his leather jacket on, obviously on his way out of the building. 'Envelope just come down from upstairs. By hand.'

'Right. Thanks, Mike. 'Night.' She reached over her desk and took the envelope from his hand. He departed with a wave.

Shannon tucked the phone receiver under her ear and punched the button to recall Alix's home number. Then she had both hands free to open the envelope from the penthouse office.

The line connected. There was the clunk of a receiver being dropped. A thick voice said, '*Mmmpghh*?'

'Alix!' Shannon grinned. 'I've got the first results down. I thought you'd want to know.'

The young woman's voice sharpened and became alert. 'Yes. Oh God. Did we do it right?'

Shannon scanned Edmund Howard's elegant copperplate hand. 'Um . . . He says he's "immensely impressed"!'

'*Yes!*' Alix sounded ecstatic.

'Listen to this.' Shannon glanced around first. There was no one at the workstations nearest her office. The place was winding down, the building would be all but empty.

She read the MD's letter into the phone. ' "I am immensely impressed with the ingenuity shown by the young woman in question. I think, despite the temporary nature of her contract, we can allow her to be part of your staff for the purposes of the

49

exercise." ' Shannon broke off. 'Well, he spotted that one.'

'He doesn't sound stupid. Not the way you described him to me.' Alix sounded anxious. 'What else does he say?'

'He says, "I am informed that your first exercise was successfully completed. A similar exercise, undertaken by a member of the *Babes!* offices, regrettably failed."'

'Failed!' Alix whooped.

Shannon adjusted the hard receiver where it pressed against her ear. She unfolded the stiff cream-coloured paper. 'There's more. Listen to this! "The *Babes!* candidate successfully began the exercise, but broke off when a message was broadcast over the PA system by mall security staff. I am reliably informed that, at two-oh-three p.m. precisely, the couple in question were publicly requested to refrain from excessive displays of physical affection—" '

Alix cheered. Shannon, hands shaking, almost dropped the phone. In an uneven voice she read on, ' "—refrain from excessive displays of physical affection, at which point the partner of the *Babes!* staff member incontinently fled, leaving the exercise uncompleted." '

'Oh . . .' Alix snuffled over the phone. 'Oh dear. Oh – *Phawww!*'

Shannon wiped her chin with the heel of her hand. Tears of laughter ran down her cheeks. She tried to catch her breath and failed. For the next few minutes, neither of the women could do anything except giggle, snuffle, and choke out 'PA system!'

'*Oh.*' Shannon wheezed. She fell back in her

chair, the letter slipping from her hand to the desk. She gripped the telephone receiver. 'Oh, poor woman!'

Alix subsided abruptly. 'God, yes. I didn't think.'

Shannon shrugged. 'That's just like Richard Stanley. He wants to win, but he doesn't quite believe women can do this. I'm willing to bet he picked on some poor girl who he knew wasn't up to it, even if only subconsciously.'

'That's awful.' Alix's voice was momentarily serious. Then she giggled again. 'But I would have liked to see it! I guess that's one up to *Femme*, then?'

'Mr Howard seems to think so.' Shannon wiped her eyes again and picked up the single sheet of paper. 'He doesn't waste any time. This letter has the next bet in it. Do you want to know what it is?'

'*Do* I?' Alix gave a sleepy midnight chuckle. 'You can't leave me in suspense until I get in to the office tomorrow morning. Tell me!'

'This is going to tax your ingenuity.' Shannon shifted around in her chair. 'You work out, don't you?'

Alix sounded bewildered. 'Sometimes. What's this got to do with anything?'

'The bet is,' Shannon read, 'that your candidate should seduce the personal trainer in a gym.'

Alix's voice brightened. 'Seduce some young guy with big pecs, you mean?'

'Uh-huh .'

'Wow. *That's* going to be a real hardship!'

'He's put down the phone numbers of some health clubs.' Shannon folded the sheet of paper and put it in the inside pocket of her jacket where it hung over the back of her office chair. 'I'll pass them on to you tomorrow.'

'Right!' Alix's smile was audible. She laughed huskily. 'I'd better get some beauty sleep, in that case. Talk to you tomorrow, Shannon.'

Shannon rested her hand on the phone receiver for a moment after the contented young woman hung up. Then, chuckling, she pushed Richard Stanley's office number.

It was picked up on the first ring. A male voice said, 'Shannon.'

'Richard. Good guess.'

'What's to guess? A bitch like you couldn't resist ringing up to gloat.'

She pictured him sitting in his office two floors above, looking out over the same view of the City. 'Richard. How unfair. I was ringing to wish your girl luck for the next one. What happened? Did you pick on some poor bimbo in your office and twist her arm?'

There was a silence. Then Richard Stanley's voice came icy and calm. 'Thank you for your best wishes, Shannon.'

'You're going to have to grit your teeth and admit a woman can be adventurous,' Shannon said. 'That is, if you want to win this contest. You'd better find an adventurous woman, hadn't you? Good night, Richard. Sweet dreams.'

He murmured, 'It isn't the end of the month yet, Shannon. Good night.'

Smirking, Shannon hung up.

After a moment, her smile faded away.

Something in Richard Stanley's tone had been – what? I don't know, she thought. Chagrin, yes, but . . . something else? Yes. A hint of I-know-something-*you*-don't-know.

But he lost. He lost. So what . . . ?

Maybe it's not him. Maybe it's just me. For some reason I'm twitchy.

Shannon stood up. Thoughtfully she pulled on her light linen jacket and picked up her briefcase.

I know what it is. I'm *envious* of Alix! *I* used to fuck like a mink. Maybe I've got old and staid and boring . . .

Shannon turned the office lights off and made the journey home.

The next working day went by in a flash. The two women had no time to do anything but exchange covert grins in passing. At four-thirty, Shannon handed Alix the phone numbers for the health clubs.

At four-forty, Alix Neville left the Midnight Rose International building.

She leapt into her car and drove away.

It was impossible to park anywhere close to the health club she had chosen.

Alix finally left her car and walked down the tree-lined suburban streets in the mid-evening sunlight. She carried her sports bag lazily by one strap, slung over her shoulder. The lipstick-pink Lycra cycle shorts and the cropped sports top she wore were quite enough in the lingering heat.

Not that it isn't a challenge, she thought as she walked. Nothing quite like guys hanging out in the gym, firming their pecs, for thinking they're God's gift to babes. Far be it from them to actually *notice* a woman. But an instructor . . . mmm. I like a man who knows what to do with his body.

Dust from the dry pavement coated her white trainers. She smelled other people's evening meals being cooked. Spices. Wine. Her own stomach was tight with excitement. Eat later, she thought. Eat afterwards.

Oh God, I'm getting hot just thinking about this!

Anticipation fluttered in her stomach. She stopped, then crossed a road junction. A car full of young guys in football strip drove past. One whistled at her through the open window. The evening air sparkled above her, dusty blue at the horizon, the sun only just thinking of going down.

She had prudently chosen one of the phone numbers away from her own district. This was a mixture of tall Edwardian houses mostly split into first-buy flats, and modern purpose-built blocks. A flat-roofed hall advertised itself, when she got close enough to read the discreet notice, as the Phoenix Sports Club.

Alix picked up her new membership card at the desk and wandered down, through pastel-green corridors with stucco classical pillars, towards the gym. The thuds and metallic clangs from beyond the double doors let her know the gym was occupied and mid-evening busy.

And I'm supposed to walk in and just say, 'Hey, let's get it together,' right on the weight-lifting machine? That'll be fun! No, I think it's: find this instructor, ask him for some special tuition, ask him for a coffee – and then *ask* him.

I hope he's at least good-looking . . .

A few minutes in the changing room and Alix felt ready to enter the gym. She walked confidently down the corridors, past the various dance studios and health and beauty rooms. An occasional voice or clatter of equipment drifted out when a door opened and shut.

Mmm?

Alix stopped, and backed up a few paces. She pushed the slightly ajar door open and peered into what turned out to be a deserted aerobics studio. Gold light gleamed in through high clerestory windows. The far end of the big room was taken up with piled mats.

The wall opposite was all one huge mirror.

Alix smiled at her own reflection. She stripped her crimson scrunchy off, whipped the silver-blonde mass of her hair through her fingers and efficiently re-affixed the tie. Her hair swung in an immense horse-tail, wisps coiling down to slide over her sleek Lycra top. In the dim light of the silent room she could see her eyes gleam.

Now wouldn't this be nice and quiet. And a mirror, too.

Alix went back to the corridor and walked on. She pushed open the gym doors, entering a low-ceilinged room that looked much bigger than it was. Mirrors made up most of the walls, reflecting weight-lifting equipment, two bulky guys bench-pressing weights, three office girls on exercycles and a man in his thirties with a shaven head banging the pecs machine. The pumping loud music was Queen.

Alix sighed. It's always Queen.

She walked over and began a warm-up on a spare mat, bending and stretching, the summer heat making her muscles easily limber. The sports equipment looked safe, she thought, if not brand-new. Nothing, however, could stop the place being irretrievably naff. And one of the bench-pressers (as she gathered from his over-loud conversation with his friend) was called Darren.

Alix sighed again.

She worked up a light sweat on the triceps machine, pulling the bar evenly down to the nape of her neck. She used only a small weight load, but her body felt pleasantly warm by the end of the sequence. She felt herself moving, muscles and tendons and ligaments, like a piece of oiled machinery. The small bulges of her biceps showed under the sleeves of her crop-top.

She swung off that machine to the cycles and pedalled energetically for a while. It was easy; she lost herself in the rhythm of movement. Smooth muscles sliding under her skin, smooth sweat trickling down her face. The burn of energy expended, legs and arms beginning to ache . . .

Alix swung down off the exercycle, aware that working out had had its usual effect. I feel randy as hell, she thought. I just want to lie down and rub a hot man all over me! But if there *is* an instructor here, I haven't seen him yet.

She exchanged a few words with one of the other women waiting to use the bench-press. Then, recalling a coin-machine down one of the corridors, she went out to get a drink, returning to the changing rooms to get some spare change from her sports bag. She picked up her watch. Six-thirty. If this place ran like any other local centre, the after-work work-outs would soon be going home to eat. The mid-evening classes would be starting.

She found the drinks machine. A soft drink hissed in her mouth, which she had not realised until then was dust-dry. She spent a few minutes looking down from a gallery into the squash courts, relishing the grunts, yelps, smashing balls, and the fact that she herself was not playing. Smiling a little, she went to find a bin for her empty can.

It was as she passed by an open door near the gym that she saw the sports centre instructor.

He was standing inside what was obviously his office, beside a desk, intently reading a sheet of paper. Alix had a minute to study him without being noticed. He wore black jogging pants and a black T-shirt, both of which looked rumpled. His hair was dark brown, nearly black, and cut militarily short. What she could see of his half-turned face gave her an impression of strong features, thick brows, and very clear brown eyes that flicked across the page in front of him.

What made him look so big, Alix realised, was not only that he was tall – and he must be well over six foot – but the fact that his muscles were extraordinarily well-defined. She let her gaze linger on his wide chest, the bulges of his shoulders, and his tendon-corded arms that sprouted unruly black hairs. His torso was neat, compact, and his thighs in the jogging pants looked muscular and firm.

Not *over*-developed, she thought. Not a muscleman. Put him in a suit and you wouldn't notice the muscles, you'd just think he's made big and strong.

Her gaze continued down, straying to the front of his close-fitting black pants and the faint bulge at the groin. Well-packed.

'Hi,' Alix said.

She leaned her shoulder up against the door of the room as she spoke. His dark gaze flicked across her in an instant: her trainers, well-filled cycle shorts and crop-top, the pony-tail of white-blonde hair, and eyes that she let go wide as he reached her face.

'Yes?' he prompted.

The first thing she noticed was that he didn't smile. His colouring was dark. That and his heavy brows and cropped hair gave him a harsh, saturnine quality. At his height he could do nothing else but look down at her – but it felt like more than that.

It feels like a challenge, Alix realised. *Right* . . . !

Maybe he gets a lot of sports bimbos chasing him. Maybe he needs someone who isn't a bimbo. And who doesn't think he's sex on a stick.

He is, though . . . Alix let her smile fade. She raked him again, head to toe, this time deliberately slowly, letting him see what she was doing. He put the piece of paper down on the desk.

'Yes?' he repeated.

'I was looking for the instructor.' Alix lifted her eyes above his waist. His gaze was level. Neutral. She added, 'I'm used to something a bit more upmarket – in the way of sports clubs.'

The big man looked at her for a long minute. He seemed to come to some decision within himself. 'I could offer you some personal tuition.'

'Are you sure you're up to it?' Alix flirted her eyebrows at him. 'Sometimes I take a lot of keeping up with.'

'Really?' His harsh expression softened when he smiled. It was a brief flash of warmth. He turned fully to face her. His movements were unhurried, but fast. Any other man, she felt, would have leaned back against the desk. This big instructor stood upright, perfectly balanced, his muscular body both relaxed and ready. Her neck ached, looking up at his face.

'Personal tuition can be strenuous,' he remarked. 'Are you sure you're in condition for it?'

'Oh, I'm exactly in condition for it,' Alix said, deadpan. 'In fact, I couldn't need it more. I'm just longing for a good, hard, exciting – work-out. Can you give it to me?'

'I'd be pleased to give it to you,' the big man said, his tone making her realise he was not entirely unaware of the double meaning. 'Have you got what it takes to really go for it?'

'Me?' Alix shifted her shoulder off the door jamb, standing upright. 'Sure. I've been told I've got a good body. Responsive. Easily trainable. You can't wear me out. You can't make me give up. If I start something, I stick with it – right to the end.'

Gravely, the big man extended a hand. 'I'm Vince.'

'Alix.' The gaping emptiness under her breast-bone pulsed as she took his hand. His big fingers enclosed her. The restrained strength of his grip left her in no doubt about how fit and strong this man was. Her pulse thudded, and her mouth went dry. She felt tight between her legs.

'You'll have to put your body in my hands, Alix,' Vince said.

'Sure.'

'Don't be so eager.' This time his saturnine face had an unmistakable smile. It made him look younger. But not any the less arrogant. 'You might not be able to take my – exercise programme.'

'I don't think you've got anything I can't handle.'

'I'll really stretch you, I promise you.'

Alix glanced around the small office, which was all but taken up by the desk and two old military-green four-drawer filing cabinets. There was no window. Fluorescent lighting gave the walls a warm yellow glow.

She reached behind herself and pulled the door to.

The lock clicked. Her fingers felt the key, and, leaning up against the door with her hands behind her back, she turned it in the lock. She remained leaning back and gazed up at Vince from under long lashes.

'So what's the warm-up?' Alix asked.

He was suddenly standing in front of her, all but touching her, and she had hardly seen him move. For a big man, he moved deftly. She could only gaze up at his face, breathing his odour of male sweat. The rise and fall of his chest brought his body within millimetres of hers.

'Something like this,' he said throatily. His palms slid up her Lycra crop-top. Her nipples sprang out and hardened, poking the stretchy material. His strong, wide-fingered hands closed around her breasts.

Without any control, she pushed herself forward into his grip. His hands were hot and dry. The silky material rasped. She reached down and pushed her fingers under the bottom of her crop-top and slid it up. He released her long enough for her to push the shocking-pink material above her breasts and for the dark-nippled globes of flesh to spring free. Then his hand closed hard over her left breast, while he bent down and his mouth clamped over her right breast. His free hand crushed her to him.

'Ohh . . . ' Alix's knees gave. His hot wet tongue

flicked expertly across her nipple. A spurt of pleasure soaked her panties in her Lycra shorts.

Her hands moved aimlessly for a moment. Then
she swallowed, hard, and began to rub his firm
chest under his black cotton T-shirt. She slipped
her fingers under the bottom of it and pushed her
hands up through the fur of his chest. He was hot,
breathing hard, and his muscles were hard-sprung.
His coiled strength tensed.

Alix put her hand down the front of his pants.

His huge erection poked out from the soft black
cloth. She knotted her fingers in the pants and
yanked them down. His cock sprang free, released
to bob against her thigh. She reached down and
wrapped her fingers around it and it leaped in her
hand.

His pants slid down to his knees. His big arm
went around her shoulders and Alix found herself
suddenly swung around, pivoting on her toes,
balance gone. He swept out with one arm. The
filing trays and the piles of paper crashed from the
desk to the floor.

Alix felt the hard edge of the desk against the
backs of her thighs. His hands grasped her shoulders and pushed her. She fell back. The smooth
surface of the desk whacked her between the
shoulder-blades. She gasped, breathless.

'Oh. *Oh!*' His hands had shifted. One thick
finger plunged into her crotch, pushing the fabric
of her tight shorts into her pussy. The silky cloth
soaked instantly. She wriggled her buttocks. She
could not get a hand down to drag her shorts and
panties off. Her body writhed, flat on her back on
the desk. She reached up, blindly grabbing at him.
She got his shoulders. He fell across her. His

weight winded her. She reached down and took his cock where it lay throbbing and engorged on her thigh, and began tantalisingly to slide her fingers up and down it. Eight solid hard inches jumped in her palm.

'Oh, girl,' the big man groaned. He still had his hand between her thighs. His musky weight crushed her. As she writhed and wriggled, his strong fingers again probed her crotch.

The Lycra of her cycle shorts slid up like a string, all but cutting her in two. Alix yelped. She felt his big hand lift her bum bodily up off the table. His other hand spanned her buttocks and clenched. The fabric pulled taut in his hand. With one swift movement, he ripped her shorts and panties down together. The garments tangled at her knees. The cool air-conditioned air struck the skin of her buttocks and the hot volcano of her sex. She thrust her hips up.

'Oh God! Stick it in me, big man! Don't wait – *do* it. Do me!'

A door banged open. A voice exclaimed, 'What the hell is going on here?'

Alix sat up sharply. She banged against the big man's chest and fell down flat again on the desk, bruising her back. She thought, agonised, *But the door is locked! I locked it myself!*

She got her head up. The door to the corridor was locked. The door behind the two filing cabinets, which she had not noticed, was open. A man in white shorts and sports shirt was gaping at her.

He was looking right up her bare fanny.

Alix squirmed frantically and uselessly, completely unable to move. The big man, Vince, looked over his shoulder. He appeared unconcerned that he was showing a pair of bare buttocks to the newcomer. 'Yes?'

'Get out of here! You filthy, perverted, vile – *out*!!'

Alix's face was hot as a furnace. She squirmed under Vince's weight. 'Let me go!'

Vince stood up and back and pulled up his jogging pants. He had his back to the open door. A huge erection poked out of the cloth. He didn't turn around but said equably, 'Sure. We're going.'

'I'm calling the police!' the man squeaked.

Alix blushed furiously. She shoved Vince away and half-fell off the desk, clawing frantically at her panties. Her thumb ripped through the lace trim. She swore. The cycle shorts clung wetly to her thighs. She heaved them up, fabric twisted and uncomfortable. 'I'm sorry! I – I'm sorry!'

'Come on, babe.' Vince folded his big hand around one of hers. With his other hand he unlocked the door to the corridor. Alix, who had had no intention of doing anything – couldn't think *what* to do – found herself irresistibly marched out of the sports club office.

'Let me go!' she snapped furiously.

The office door banged shut behind them. She heard a voice behind the door, and the jangle of a phone. One leg of her shorts was twisted right around. She half-hopped down the corridor, look-ing vainly for the signs to the ladies' changing rooms.

'Hey, babe.' The big man's hand on her shoulder turned her around. She felt his palm flat against his back. Alix sprawled against his muscled body. She felt wooden flooring under a bare foot – one of her trainers was missing. Fallen off? In the office?

Her face flamed. 'How *could* you?'

'Like this.' Vince thrust his other hand down her crop-top and grabbed one breast. To her anger, it swelled instantly in his hand. He jerked his head at the deserted aerobics studio across the corridor. 'Looks pretty quiet in there. I'm not finished yet. Nor are you. I don't like to see a lady needing to come and not do something about it. So what about it?'

Alix grabbed his wrist. Her hand wouldn't even close round its girth. She dragged his hand out of her cleavage. 'I will not! That guy looked *straight up me!* That was so *embarrassing!* My knickers are wet! I want to die! And you're asking me if I want to shag you in front of the mirrors? No! No. No!'

He said something else but she didn't hear it. Face flaming, she ran down the corridor. She didn't stop in the changing rooms. A brief tug on her shorts only ripped the crotch.

'Oh, *shit!*' Alix threw her bag across the changing rooms. A motherly woman looked out from a cubicle, startled.

'You alright, love?'

'*Fine.*' She retrieved her bag. It contained nothing else for her to wear.

Alix Neville stormed out of the Phoenix Sports Club into the open air. She stomped up the road, clutching the bag to her crotch, one bare foot black with the pavement's dust, her face flaming red as fire. It took her three-quarters of an hour to find where she had parked her car.

Shannon Garrett emerged from studying a stack of glossy photos to see Richard Stanley in the doorway of her office.

'Good morning,' the *Babes!* editor murmured. His blond hair was neatly brushed and his Armani suit spotless. Shannon, who had spent a sweaty hour driving into the office from west London, glared at him.

'Yes?' she said.

'Just dropped round to offer you my condolences,' Richard said, pale blue eyes slightly glassy. Probably been out celebrating, Shannon thought sourly.

She kept her voice low, so as not to be overheard outside the office. 'I take it you've been notified that our attempt this time was a failure.'

'Oh yes,' Richard smiled thoughtfully. 'I had a word with Edmund.'

I bet you don't call him 'Edmund' when he's around, Shannon thought. I bet it's *sir, Mr Howard, sir!*

'Not only did your attempt count as a failure,' Richard went on. 'As my competitor was quite happy to carry on, *Babes!* has been deemed to have won this bet.'

Shannon pushed her curly red-brown hair back from her face. She gave the man in front of her her full attention. Bewildered, she said, '*Your* competitor?'

'Yes. Quite a coincidence, but it seems they both picked the same health club off that list of phone numbers.' Richard inspected his manicured nails.

Unguardedly, Shannon said, 'Alix didn't mention any other women there.'

'No.' Richard stared around her tiny office, and finally returned his gaze to her. His grin widened. 'My *man* didn't actually mention that he *wasn't* the

65

gym instructor . . .'

'You what?' Shannon said dangerously.

'Nothing in the bet said I had to pick a woman. Just one of my staff. Sexual equality, after all . . .' Her rival editor smirked. 'He's a real find, is Vince Russell. He's our security man – he handles the security desk for the *Babes!* offices. Ex-army, before he joined us. You might say he's used to being adventurous.'

'A thug,' Shannon said bitterly. 'An ex-squaddie thug.'

Richard Stanley smiled. 'But *Babes!*'s thug, nevertheless . . . Vince realised who the girl must be, of course, almost instantly. So he just let her think that he was – who she thought he was. And he was more than willing to carry things through to a finish! But your girl wasn't. I guess that's round two to *Babes!*. And it's the twenty-first of the month today . . .'

Chapter Six

EDMUND HOWARD ENTERED his penthouse office just as the sun rose out of the Thames mists. From this height, through the floor-length office windows, he could see all Canary Wharf laid out below him. The view extended as far down river as the QEII Bridge, lost in the eastern dazzle.

He did not carry a briefcase and his Burberry coat was held loosely over one arm. With the harsh sunlight illuminating his features he looked like a mountain crag, hard and ancient and strong. His startlingly blue eyes narrowed, very slightly, as he looked around his office.

A young woman leaned back against his mahogany desk. Her hands were behind her, supporting her. His gaze travelled up her slender long bare legs, to the slightly thrust-forward bodice of her brown silk shirt-dress. The silk clung, stretched taut between her rounded breasts.

Edmund Howard frowned. He looked up.

A very cheerful and entirely unseductive brat's grin met his gaze.

'Neville,' the young woman said. She shifted her

behind off his desk and offered her hand for him to shake. 'Alix Neville. I'd be very surprised if you don't know who I am, Mr Howard.'

'Ms Neville.' Edmund Howard took her hand and held it for a moment. Her skin was smooth-textured, a little cool with the office's air-conditioning. Her palm felt dry. With an impulse of old-fashioned gallantry, he raised her hand and kissed it. Then he walked around behind his desk, dropping his coat over the leather sofa on the way with the gesture of a much younger man.

'Even if Security had not told me you were waiting,' he said gravely, 'I could hardly not be aware of the magnificent Ms Neville. Your winning performance in the atrium was . . . entrancing.'

At that, her strongly defined eyebrows lifted. Her silver hair spilled over her shoulders, caught up at her ears with softwood combs. She grinned at him again, this time ruefully. 'Yesterday was a lot *less* entertaining.'

'Ah . . .' Edmund Howard leaned back in his polished wooden chair. He steepled his fingers and studied the girl over his strong, manicured nails. She looked younger than the age his security dossier gave her; hardly into her twenties. Bright-eyed and long-legged, moving with a gamine sexiness that was redeemed by her expression. *No*, he thought, satisfied, confirming his change of opinion; *not just another bimbo*.

'Your experience with Mr Vincent Russell?' he prompted, not needing to call up the file on-screen to refresh his memory.

The young woman looked at him sardonically. 'We didn't get as far as last names. And – before you ask – no, Shannon Garrett *isn't* aware that I'm here.'

'Please do sit down. I'll order tea.' He thumbed a key, confident that no matter how early he might arrive in his office, his personal staff would be there before him. A very few moments later, he was proved right by the arrival of his PA, a grave young man, carrying a tray of Earl Grey tea and cinnamon toast.

'Hold my calls,' Edmund Howard murmured. The PA removed himself unobtrusively.

Alix Neville ignored the wooden chair on the far side of his desk. She swiped a slice of toast from the tray and sat on the leather sofa, bare legs curled under her. Her hair fell to one side. He had a glimpse of the nape of her neck, where fine fair tendrils curled over the dimpled indentations of her spine. She looked, for a moment, very young indeed.

'My dear, if you don't wish to continue with this, I assure you that you need not. The wager means that, by definition, there can be no compulsion involved.' Edmund Howard smiled. His harsh features gave his smile a sinister undertone.

The young woman looked up and met his gaze. Her eyes were brilliant, and grey as rainwater. 'The bet's about being adventurous. About *liking* being adventurous. I know that. Did I look as though I wasn't enjoying myself with Simon?'

The security-camera videos of Alix in the lift had been explicitly clear. He remembered watching them. He shifted a little in his chair. A warmth flowered in his groin. He leaned forward at the desk. Under the desktop, his cock stirred in his expensive light wool suit trousers. 'But if you're enjoying the competition, Ms Neville, why are you here?'

Butter from the cinnamon toast ran down her fingers. She lifted her hand and licked the grease from her skin, the pink tip of her tongue dipping into the crevices between her fingers. Absently, she wiped her half-clean hand down her bare calf, leaving a shine on the smooth skin. Her eyes fixed on him. Her eyebrows dinted, as if a thought occurred to her.

The young woman switched her legs off the sofa to the thickly carpeted floor. She smoothed the slinky deep-brown silk of her shirt-dress down over her knees. She took a determined deep breath before speaking, her shoulders went back, and the vee of her dress filled with the swell of her breasts. 'I mean, I *guess* they didn't cheat. No one said the bet was *only* about women . . .'

Edmund Howard coughed. He brushed absently at his expertly barbered silver-grey hair. Under cover of the movement, he shifted his legs under the desk. His hardening erection sprang up, tangled in his underpants, and strained against the fabric at his crotch.

'More tea?' he said.

'Tea? Tea. Oh – *tea*. Yes. Thank you.' Alix Neville gave him a distracted look as he leaned forward to pour a cup and then push the tray into her reach. She had an expression of puzzlement that made her face foxy and sharp. She looked as though she had momentarily forgotten the purpose of her visit.

He savoured the taste of the tea on his tongue, gazing out of the office window. The day outside was already becoming heated. Men carried their summer suit jackets, walking towards steel and chrome buildings below. The offices of Midnight

Rose International were filling up for the day's work.

'I think I know what you're going to say.' Edmund Howard turned in his chair at last. The young woman sat now with her hands clasped over her silk-clad knees, watching him with cool, clear eyes. He added, 'And I believe that I agree with you. These . . . bets . . . were intended to find out what people are capable of *enjoying*. My caprice in this matter was not intended to cause humiliation or pain to anyone. Mr Russell and Mr Stanley seem not to have played the last bet entirely fairly – or in the spirit of the game. I think you are correct. I shall hand the matter over to Accounts, and abide by their decision as to whether *Femme* or *Babes!* survives.'

Alix Neville said, 'No.'

Startled, Edmund Howard leaned back again in his chair. Her flat contradiction put harsh lines into his face. He frowned. He was not aware how cold his blue eyes became, or how unused he had become to being questioned.

' "No"?'

The young woman got to her feet, scrambling up out of the leather sofa. He caught a glimpse of the flimsy, chocolate-brown lacy panties under her dress as the silk hem pulled up. She stood with a poise and balance that had something dazzling about it, the sun through the office windows catching her silver hair. And then she laughed.

'Sorry. I'm usually more tactful where Big Bosses are concerned – especially when I'm telling them why their junk computer networks don't work. I meant, "I'd really rather you didn't, sir".'

Her cool eyes twinkled as she said *sir*. Edmund

Howard could not prevent himself smiling.

'Really?'

'Let the bet stand,' Alix Neville appealed. Her expression seemed serious, but her eyes shone bright with humour and excitement. 'That's what I came to ask you. I can be adventurous – I was *so bored* before I started doing this! I don't want to stop. But,' she added, 'I want to show this Vince Russell just *how* adventurous things can get. You can understand that, can't you?'

Edmund Howard studied her. A slender woman, tall and long-legged, with strength readily apparent. It was the roused, angry light in her eye that made him smile, finally, and say, 'I'm a competitive man myself, Ms Neville. *I* don't like to lose a bet either. You imagine that Mr Stanley will continue to put Mr Russell forward as his competitor?'

'I think you'd have to hit him over the head with a baseball bat to stop him,' Alix said frankly. 'I'm going to show Vince Russell a thing or two, Mr Howard. I'm probably going to do that *anyway*. But I'd just as soon that it helped Shannon keep *Femme* on the newsstands. Will you do it? Will you keep the bet going?'

'A competition in – adventurousness – between yourself and Mr Russell?' he said thoughtfully. 'It could be seen as a reasonable part of the bet, I suppose. If you're sure.'

'Hey, I'm *sure*. Watch me.' She grinned the small, crooked grin again. 'You will watch me, won't you, Mr Howard?'

The flirt of her silver eyebrows caught him entirely unprepared. His subsiding erection suddenly swelled and throbbed, taut again against his clothes.

'Very well. The bet continues.' He looked impassively away from her. 'I shall send a message down to Ms Garrett when I have devised the next contest for you and Mr Russell.'

Edmund Howard did not watch the young woman leave. He heard the office door close softly behind her. Carefully he unscrewed the cap of his gold fountain pen and drew a sheet of heavy embossed paper towards him across the desk.

He did not write immediately. He sat and gazed out of the window, the summer sun bright on his face. Ms Neville. And Mr Russell. Who must attempt the same bet . . .

'What a pity,' he murmured, 'that Mr Russell is involved. If not, I should be very inclined to make the next bet *Seduce the Managing Director of Midnight Rose International*. Sadly, that seems to be outside the spirit of the game as well. Now . . .'

His fountain pen began to scratch decisively on the creamy paper.

Shannon Garrett leaned forward towards the office restroom mirror, slicking on an almost invisible film of crushed-strawberry lipgloss. The rest of her make-up was equally subtle: a hint of earth-colours to bring out her striking hazel eyes. Her copper-brown curls swung as she leaned back, blotting with a tissue, satisfied.

The mirror dazzled, surrounded as it was by a hoop of bare opaque light-bulbs. Shannon suspected the building's designer of being a frustrated Hollywood actor. She gave a last glance at her reflection. Behind her, in the mirror, the restroom door opened.

'Alix.' She turned round and gazed at the

younger woman. Flustered, Shannon stammered, 'I had the memo down – about yesterday – I'm terribly sorry . . .'

Alix Neville's cheeks turned pink. 'Don't worry about it. It won't happen again.'

'I can understand that you don't want to do any more of this . . .' Shannon moved back. It was that or be walked through as the younger woman strode forward to the mirror, dropped her tiny clutch-bag onto the sink surround and pulled out a wide-toothed comb.

'It won't happen again.' Alix ran cold water on her wrists. After a second she turned off the tap, picked up the comb and yanked furiously at her masses of silver-blonde hair. 'Because next time will be entirely different. You'll see.'

'"Next time"? You mean you're going to carry on with this?'

'Damn right I am!' The young woman's eyes, in the mirror, met Shannon's gaze. 'Do we know what the next bet is?'

'Not yet. The memo said he'd notify me within the next twenty-four hours. Look . . .' Shannon turned around and leaned her buttocks back against the sink surround so that she could look at Alix instead of Alix's reflection. A few spatters of water from the sink marked the front of the young woman's well-filled silk dress. A single drop of water trickled down her slim wrist as she raised her hands to pull up her hair at the sides and fasten it with combs. Her expression was pure determination.

'Maybe I could help,' Shannon suggested quietly.

'*You?*'

Alix's tone stung her. Shannon snapped, 'Yes. Me. What's so amazing about that?'

Alix darted a glance towards the mirror. 'Oh – nothing.'

Shannon turned, looking at their reflections side by side. She suddenly noticed that Alix's clear-skinned face wore no make-up. And she did not have even the beginnings of laughter-lines. Her young breasts were taut and firm and bra-less under her silk shirt-dress.

'So let me help you out with the next bet,' Shannon repeated quietly.

'No way!'

'Fine.' Shannon Garrett picked up her canvas handbag. 'Fine. If that's the way you want it – I'll be in touch as soon as I hear from upstairs.'

She let the restroom door fall shut behind her, cutting off a remark from Alix Neville.

How dare she! Just because she's a kid in her twenties! I suppose she thinks I wouldn't be any good at this. I suppose she thinks I can't do it. I suppose *she* thinks I'm too old. What a *nerve*!

Sheer fury powered her through the day, making Julia Royston's life a fast-forward nightmare. By four in the afternoon, Shannon stared at a desk momentarily clear of work.

'If anyone wants me, I'm picking up my car from its service!' She slammed her office door behind her. A pile of old issues of *Femme* fell off a shelf and thudded to the carpet. She ignored them and walked to the lift. Behind her, the *Femme* office staff breathed a collective sigh of relief.

Shannon rammed the heel of her hand onto the lift-call button.

Too old! Goddammit, I'll *show* her *too old*!

Her taxi dropped her at the corner of the East End street. The pastel sky above the railway arches blurred with pollution that tanged faintly on Shannon's tongue. Above her, a few stems of goldenrod grew out of the Victorian brickwork and craned towards the hazy summer sun, yellow flowers blazing. A mosaic of red and blue paint graffitied the walls. Shannon walked down towards the garage workshop under the first archway, keeping to the minimal shadow on the pavement. Sweat trickled down the back of her neck.

One of the garage doors stood open. The wood's green paint was blistered and pale. A radio blared inside. Shannon stepped cautiously across the threshold. Going from the hot street to the comparatively dark workshop left her dazzled. She squinted into the hot twilight and raised her voice over the music. 'Hello? Anyone here?'

The sound-level dipped as an unseen hand turned down the radio. Shannon's eyes began to adjust to the shade. She watched a bare-armed mechanic in oil-stained overalls and nothing else walk forward from between glints of chrome and paintwork – cars in various degrees of disassembly.

'Ms Garrett. The BMW?' The mechanic's voice was low, husky. 'I've done the service. It's through in the yard. It'll be easier if you drive it out the back way.'

'Sure,' Shannon said. The sunlight from the street glowed on the garage floor. Oil-cans, racks of tools, and shiny wall-calendars caught the light.

Shannon could see clearly now. The mechanic smiled at her. Medium-tall, skinny, with long blonde hair tied back with a neckerchief – a woman, Shannon realised. The oil-stained dungaree straps crossed slender, tanned shoulders. As the mechanic turned aside to a bench, hunting through paperwork for Shannon's bill, she saw the front of the dungarees fall forward far enough to disclose the curve of a breast, skin glowing pale in the dim workshop.

Shannon's face felt suddenly hot. She rummaged in her bag for her chequebook. 'You're new, aren't you? I didn't know there was a woman mechanic working here.'

'Donna.' The woman thrust a hand forward. Now Shannon could see her clearly – she was in her late twenties. She wore rope-soled sandals, moving sure-footedly over the oily concrete. 'I started last week. You got problems with a woman doing this?'

Shannon shook hands. Donna's grip was firm.

'Good grief, no!' Shannon laughed.

Donna smiled in response. Her mouth was large, full; her lower lip red in the gloom. 'Yeah, good. I've been getting lip from some of the guys. That'll wear off. Give 'em time.'

'I don't imagine it's easy being in this kind of job.'

Shannon's gaze fell on one of the wall-calendars. Nearly naked women in Lycra crop-tops and cut-off shorts pressed weights in a gym, the photography clearly bringing out the patches of sweat between their breasts and the sheen on their smooth thighs and bare stomachs. 'You must find some of this pin-up stuff offensive.'

'No.' Donna looked her firmly in the eye. 'Anyway, that one's mine.'

Shannon glanced again at the calendar. *August* had sweat-wet tendrils of hair sticking to her neck and clinging to the smooth skin of her collar-bones. 'I go to the gym sometimes. I don't see many like her . . .'

'Shame.' Donna grinned. 'Your car's out the back, Ms Garrett. This way.'

The heavy cloth of the dungarees slid across the young woman's body as she turned, pulling tight for a second over her slim buttocks. Shannon felt a growing warmth. She ran a finger under the boat-necked collar of her linen dress. Sweat prickled the tops of her breasts and under her arms. It was more than the heat of the vehicle-filled workshop causing it, she knew.

I couldn't, Shannon thought. I don't have time. I have to get back to the office. And I don't know that this Donna is even interested . . .

A little voice in Shannon's mind said, *She might be – what if she is?*

'Nonsense!' She realised she'd spoken aloud. The background music from the radio covered her lapse. Putting the cheque down on the workbench, Shannon walked through the garage and out into the back yard.

Sun dazzled her. Bright light gleamed back from the windscreens of the ranks of parked cars. Donna bent down near a standpipe tap, coiling a hose away. Lather and water on the concrete rapidly evaporated in the heat.

Shannon picked out her red BMW, parked close to the high concrete wall at the back of the yard. With the railway arch behind and the walls around the yard, they could not be observed. The steel-barred yard gate was closed.

'Ah . . . the chrome,' Shannon said. Donna straightened up and looked at her. Shannon added an explanation. 'The bumpers could do with a bit of a clean. Could you do that? I wouldn't mind waiting.'

The blonde woman stretched her bare arms in the heat. 'Oh . . . sure, why not? Nothing else is due in until five. I'll do it now.'

Donna reached up and unsnapped the clip of her dungaree-strap. The strap slid off her bare, tanned shoulder. Her hand went up to the other strap. 'It's too hot for overalls. I do the car washes like this. You don't mind?'

The front of her dungarees fell down. A jade-green spaghetti-strap bikini top became visible, straining to contain her large, round, tanned breasts. Donna eased her heavy dungarees down, unfastening the metal buttons at the side. Shannon watched as a lithe, tanned stomach came into view. The woman pushed the dungarees down off her hips and turned, standing on one leg to kick the garment off. A tiny jade-green bikini bottom cupped her neat, taut buttocks.

'I don't mind,' Shannon said without thinking. 'You go right ahead, I'll just enjoy the view.'

She blushed. Her naturally pale skin must be red now. Her faint freckles would be hidden in the flush. She dropped her gaze from the woman's gold-brown eyes.

'That's okay,' Donna's voice said. 'That's fine. I like an audience.'

It wouldn't count towards the bets. It wouldn't do anything for *Femme*.

But it might just do a lot for *me. Too old*, indeed!

Shannon moved into the sparse shade of the workshop rear door. She looked at Donna, but the young woman had turned away towards the standpipe tap. Her hand went up to tug the kerchief and a mass of gold-blonde hair fell halfway down her slender, curving back.

The jade-green bikini top tied at the back with strings. What would it be like, Shannon thought, if I just walked over there and gave those strings a quick tug . . . ?

A sudden pulse of heat flowered between her legs. Shannon shifted from foot to foot. She smoothed the linen dress over her bottom and perched herself on the wing of a green Jaguar parked near the workshop doors. Trying desperately to seem unconcerned, she glanced over towards Donna.

The mechanic bent over, filling a bucket. The triangle of cloth pulled taut across her tanned buttocks. She kicked off the rope-soled sandals and Shannon saw she had a tiny blue butterfly tattooed on her foot. Donna straightened up, holding the bucket of soapy water and a cloth. She walked across to the front of the BMW without looking at Shannon and bent down to soap the chrome. The swell of her full breasts pressed into her bikini top. Shannon stared straight down the tanned, shadowed cleavage.

'Hot, ain't it?' Donna straightened up. Her forearms dripped soapy water onto the concrete. She flicked a quick glance at Shannon and the corners of her lips curved irresistibly into a smile. 'Let me wash this down.'

She walked across to the standpipe and hose.

Her long brown legs gleamed in the sun. The skin of her calves and thighs was golden-brown, flawless. She swung her hips very slightly as she went, the metal clips holding the bikini strings at hip and breast flashing silver in the sun.

'Too hot . . .' Her strong hand twisted the tap. A jet of water shot out of the hose that she held. Donna raised her head and looked straight at Shannon. She held one hand in the sparkling jet for a moment, then wiped her face with her wet hand. '*Much* too hot for work . . .'

'Yes.' Shannon's voice dried up. Adrenaline pumped through her body. Her skin shivered with it and she felt dizzy. She squirmed where she sat on the hot metalwork of the Jaguar. The thin cotton of her panties rode up into her aroused sex. She wriggled her hips. The woman stared straight at her lap.

'Yeah . . .' Donna gripped the neck of the hosepipe. A silver jet of water only trickled now, spattering on the cracked concrete. 'Well, I'm hot . . .'

Shannon watched the woman lift the hosepipe above her head. The shower of water dampened Donna's hair. It shone brown-blonde in the sun as the water soaked her. Trickles of water ran down her neck. Still with her eyes fixed on Shannon, Donna passed the nozzle of the hose across her bare shoulders. Water ran down her neck, pouring down over her breasts, spilling down into the deep cleft between them. With her free hand, she pulled open one bikini-cup and directed the stream of water into it. The jade-green material soaked, dark green patches appearing and merging, until her whole bikini top stretched, wet and dripping, across her big breasts.

'I could cool you down,' Donna said huskily. 'Or make you hot.'

Donna's free hand dropped to the front of her bikini bottom. She pulled the top of the triangle of material forward and thrust the nozzle of the hose inside. The fabric immediately darkened. A cascade of cool water poured down the woman's crotch and thighs, pooling at her feet.

'Cool or hot, your choice . . .'

Shannon swallowed. Her breath came short. Almost without volition, her hands went down against the hot metal of the Jaguar and pushed her up onto her feet. Her knees felt rubbery.

'Cool *and* hot.' Shannon staggered forward on unsteady legs. Heat throbbed in her groin. She reached the place where Donna stood. The sun beat down on her head. 'I want both, and I want it *now.*'

Donna's gold-brown eyes stared into hers. The younger woman did not smile now. A flush darkened her cheeks. She licked her lower lip, moistness glistening in the sun.

Shannon put both her arms around the woman. Her bare skin touched the wet, tanned skin of the other and the soaking cloth of the bikini. Carefully she took the hose from Donna's hand, brought it round behind them and tucked the nozzle down the back of Donna's bikini-pants. A flood of cool water poured across Donna's buttocks and down her legs. She squealed and wriggled as it flooded her crotch.

'Cool and hot,' Shannon gasped. She put her free hand on the woman's back and pressed her close. They stood clamped together, embracing, the wet cloth soaking Shannon's linen dress. Soaking her to the skin.

Shannon dropped the hose, took Donna's shoulders in her hands and plunged her face between the swelling curves of her big breasts, kissing her frantically. The wet skin under her lips tasted salty with sweat, tangy with the scent of oil. She dragged one bikini-cup aside and clamped her mouth over the young woman's nipple. Donna's flesh filled her mouth, firm and warm. Shannon sucked and licked, frantic to get her mouth over all of Donna, both hands kneading the firm globes of flesh. 'You're so big – you're too much woman for me—!'

'I'm just enough woman for you,' Donna growled. Her arms tensed. Under the smooth tanned skin, Shannon felt muscle. The garage mechanic clamped her hands around Shannon, pinning her arms to her side, and lifted her feet off the ground. Shannon felt herself carried back until the bonnet of the green Jaguar caught her behind the knees. She sprawled on her back across the hot painted metal. The sun dazzled her, and the smell of oil and petrol filled her nostrils; wiped out a second later by the musky scent of Donna's body.

'I said I'd clean the *car*.' The young woman's eyes gleamed with mischief. 'But I don't mind doing the owner.'

Shannon sprawled helplessly on her back, the car bonnet hard under her shoulder-blades and buttocks. Donna's hand dipped and came up holding the plastic bucket. Shannon saw it lifted and upended. A cascade of soapy water hit her squarely in the neck of her linen dress. The almost-cold water shocked her skin alive and tingling.

'Ohhh!'

Donna's hands cupped her breasts under the wet linen dress. Her fingers closed around them and squeezed tight. Shannon gasped. Her nipples hardened and her breasts swelled. In her cotton panties, her labia engorged and throbbed. She reached down and thrust both her hands down the front of Donna's bikini-pants. The warm, taut belly quivered under her fingers. She thrust her fingers further in, finding curling damp hair. Her finger-tips shocked against a white-hot wet heat in Donna's cleft.

'Oh, *yeah* . . .' Donna's hands stayed clamped to Shannon's breasts. She yanked the neck of the linen dress down. Shannon's skin tingled as silk-warm air flowed over her naked breasts. She plunged her fingers into Donna's pulsing vagina.

'Yes!' Donna dropped her head and fastened her mouth on Shannon's breast. Her long wet hair fell over Shannon's bare shoulders. The licking and sucking took Shannon away on a dizzy, plunging adrenaline ride.

Shannon stiffened three fingers and pushed up hard. Donna gasped; her mouth full. Shannon's nipple jutted. The slick wetness of Donna's sex tightened and released on Shannon's hand. She clamped her free hand to the woman's buttocks, trapping Donna against her sprawled body. Deeper, deeper, working up a rhythm – Donna's head lifted. Her whole body pounded and heaved, breathless. 'Oh God, fuck me, fuck me!'

Air stung cool on Shannon's saliva-covered breasts. She half hauled herself upright, stiff fingers thrusting up, up, up. Her free hand cupped Donna's tight little bum, yanking the cloth down, hand against naked skin. Shannon lifted her face and buried it between Donna's hot, flushed breasts.

'Ohhhh!!' Donna's sex loosened and flooded. She threw her head back as she came, gold hair flashing in the sun. 'Oh God, oh God, oh God, yes . . .'

The slim, strong body sprawled hot and limp over Shannon, pressing her down onto the Jaguar's bonnet. Wet hair tangled across Shannon's face. She lifted her hands and began to caress the sides of Donna's full breasts, where the young woman lay face-down on top of her, chest heaving, breathless.

'That was quite something,' Shannon murmured.

Donna's head lifted. Her arching dark eyebrows rose mischievously. 'Sure it was. But I ain't done yet.'

Skin to sweaty skin, Donna began slowly to slide down Shannon's body until her bare feet touched the concrete. Shannon slumped back. The dazzling blue sky filled her eyes. From inside the workshop, the radio played languorous pop music.

She felt a hand grip the hem of her linen dress. Then another hand. Before she could move, her dress was jerked up over her hips. The hot metal of the car stung her buttocks, encased in her thin wet panties. She raised her head. 'Donna . . .'

'Didn't I tell you I'm not finished yet?'

Shannon watched the young woman slide down until she knelt on the concrete in front of the car. The sun prickled hot against Shannon's bare stomach, thighs and calves.

Cool hands pressed against the inside of her

thighs, gently but insistently urging them apart. 'Come on, babe . . .'

Shannon spread her legs obediently. She let her head fall back and gazed up at the sky. She closed her eyes. The sun's brightness turned her vision shadowed and private.

Delicate fingers stroked her thighs. She felt her skin flush. Slowly the fingertips inched up until they pushed under the edge of her panties. Teasingly slow, she felt her panties pulled down. Her sex throbbed, unsatisfied. She moaned in the back of her throat and wriggled her hips, squirming her body up towards Donna.

A hot, wet tongue trailed up her thigh, around the bush of her damp hair and over the slim curve of her belly. Shannon gave a throaty growl. Her body arched. The tongue dipped, teasingly, playing with the roots of her pubic hair. She groped with a hand, found Donna's head, and pushed it down into her crotch. 'Please . . .'

'Oh, you're coming, babe. You're coming . . .'

Donna's hard tongue thrust straight up into her sex. Shannon screamed with the pleasure of the sensation. Her body writhed, spread-eagled across the car, legs as wide as she could stretch them. Two hands clamped on her bare hips. The tongue swirled around her cleft, tongue-tip flicking her clit. Her back arched shudderingly. She arched tight as a drawn bow. 'Now! Now!'

Donna's tongue jabbed, flickeringly. The hot walls of Shannon's sex dripped, throbbing in anticipation. The woman's heated moist breath feathered her skin and her bush of hair. Shannon clenched her fists, pleading. 'Now!'

The woman's hot tongue jabbed her cleft. A full-lipped mouth settled over her clit and sucked. At the same moment, smooth curved fingers jammed themselves up into Shannon's sex, so hard and firm she felt completely filled. Poised on the edge of unbearable sensation, her whole body froze.

Donna's tongue softened, caressingly licking at Shannon's swollen clit. Donna's small hand stirred, drew back—

'Oh yes,' Shannon gasped, 'do me, do me now, oh God, *do* it!'

Donna's fingers thrust up into her.

Shannon came helplessly, convulsively, buttocks lifting right up off the car metalwork, yelling ecstatically. 'Oh, yes, *yes* . . .'

The woman mechanic's strong arm drew back, thrust forward again, and Shannon lost the world again in a skin-shivering, sweating, mind-blowing explosion of pleasure.

The sultry evening heat beat back from the brick walls of Shannon's tiny back garden. Shannon sprawled in a relaxer chair, drinking white wine and soda, looking up at the evening sky through the creamy petals of the flowers on the magnolia. A flicker of heat-lightning stalked the invisible London horizon beyond the garden walls. It's going to rain, she thought, and then: who's that?

The faint doorbell *was* hers, she decided. She padded lazily barefoot through the house to the front door and opened it. Alix Neville stood on the step.

'Oh. Alix. I . . .'

Alix interrupted. 'Can't stay long. I'm on my way somewhere. I thought you might want to see this.'

Shannon glanced at the folded piece of paper that was held out to her. Cream-coloured heavy paper, written over in an elegant fine hand . . . Edmund Howard's handwriting.

I forgot! she thought, aghast. I forgot to go into the office again after I collected the car. This is it. This is the next bet!

'Thanks – sorry.' Shannon stood back. 'I'm sorry. Come in. Let me read this.'

Alix Neville walked past her into the tiny hallway. The young woman was wearing a knee-length pale gold microfibre raincoat, despite the evening's heat. As she brushed past Shannon, Shannon felt a hard obstruction of some kind under it, at the younger woman's hip. She followed Alix into the main room, eyes still on the paper.

'Good Lord.' Shannon read it again. 'Are you sure you want to do this?'

Shannon gazed at the young woman. Alix's silver-blonde hair was plaited, wound, and fastened up in a tight topknot. Her foxy face was alive with excitement. 'Are you kidding? This'll give me Vince Russell right where I want him!'

Shannon nodded slowly, understanding clearly now. 'You've got a score to settle with him, haven't you?'

Alix grinned. 'That's why I don't need any help. It's nothing personal. It's just that I want to do this one myself. Oh boy, do I want to . . . !'

'I see.'

'I mean, I thought you seemed a bit pissed off about something, in the Ladies' at lunch-time.' The young woman shrugged. 'But I guess you weren't. I was mistaken. Anyway, I thought you'd better know what the bet was. And you can wish me luck for tonight – not that I'm going to need it!'

Shannon Garrett smoothed her shortie Chinese silk robe down over her thighs. Body tingling, she recalled the hours after she left the office in what she had to admit had, at the time, been a fit of pique. Shannon giggled. Now that's what I *call* a service . . .

'Shannon?' Alix asked, quizzically.

'Annoyed? Me? No,' Shannon said expansively. She chuckled again. 'Not in the least. I'm fine. You go ahead. Best of luck, Alix. And I want to hear all about it!'

The lightweight raincoat rustled as Alix Neville tugged the belt more tightly around her slim waist. Her cool eyes lifted, and Shannon met her gaze. The younger woman licked her full lower lip.

'The twenty-first, isn't it? There isn't much of the month left to go,' Alix said. '*Femme* needs to be one ahead, don't we? Don't worry. I don't intend to lose twice. I'm going through with this bet!'

The front door clicked shut. Shannon listened to Alix's high heels tapping away down the pavement, then walked back out into her garden. The drone of bees and traffic filled the soft air, and the warmth from the creeper-covered bricks glowed against her skin.

She looked down at the sheet of paper in her hand. This time there was nothing on it but a single address. She studied the name written above it: *Pleasure Bound*.

Chapter Seven

IF SHE HAD expected anything, Alix realised, it had been an address somewhere in one of the seedier parts of south London. Little run-down Victorian terraces with 1960s' concrete-and-glass community halls, and a back room up a flight of stairs above the dustbins.

Not *this*.

Alix pulled a ten-pound note out of her raincoat pocket for the taxi. The black cab driver thanked her as he drove off into the back streets around Sloane Square.

Alix straightened her shoulders and took a deep breath. Plush brick 1930s' apartment blocks towered up into the evening sky, above neat streets. The address on the card proved to be a few yards away, in a building opposite an extremely high-class antiques shop window. The house was four storeys high, with tall Georgian windows and a smart wash of cream paint. She walked up the steps. A discreet brass plaque beside the door read *Pleasure Bound: Members Only. Ring.*

Alix obediently rang.

The door opened almost immediately. Alix had

been staring over her shoulder at the last light of sunset settling green over the rooftops with a promise of welcome rain. She turned and found herself facing an elegant woman with grey hair in a chignon, wearing an understated Versace dress.

'I'm Alix Neville,' Alix said coolly, determined not to be intimidated. She held out the embossed black-and-silver card.

The woman studied it for a moment. Her thin lips curved into a welcoming smile. 'Ah, of course. One of Edmund's friends. Do come in, my dear. Now, I'm Natalie. I shall be overseeing your entertainment this evening, and if there's anything that you want – anything – in addition to our normal fare, you must let me know. We can be innovative if required. We'll do our very best to make sure that you are completely satisfied.'

'Of course. Thank you.' Alix walked past Natalie into the lobby. A cream-coloured carpet covered the floor, and the walls were a pale gold. A picture in a plain frame caught her eye as she walked past, and she stopped, the older woman stopping behind her as she did so.

'Is that . . . ?'

'A previous guest, my dear. A very talented one, too, I may say.'

Alix looked up at the painting where it hung above a small spotlight. All the background was darkness. A single figure was illuminated, as if under a moonlit window. A woman with blue-black hair drawn tightly back from her aristocratic face and bound up in a braid coronet. She had not been painted smiling. Her aquiline features were cold, self-possessed, and her slightly almond-shaped green eyes entirely in control.

Below her head, from neck to feet, the woman was clad in a skin-tight leather body-suit. It strained to enclose her thrusting breasts and stretched taut across her hips. A thick leather belt was strapped about her, steel rings attached to it. From one ring hung a short-thonged whip. Her boots were tight, thigh-high, and had six-inch spike heels. The plaque under the portrait read: *Mistress Raven*.

A curious sensation fluttered in the pit of Alix's stomach. She forced her gaze away from the woman in the painting, back to Natalie.

'Welcome to *Pleasure Bound*,' Natalie said. She held up her slender hand, opening the fingers slightly in a gesture towards the painting. 'Would you prefer to meet her or to *be* her?'

Alix smiled.

'I would prefer to be her,' she said. 'I'm expecting a friend here later this evening. I'd like it to be a little surprise for him.'

Natalie nodded with an expression of perfect understanding. 'Of course. I assume he would wish to be delivered to you . . . involuntarily, as it were.'

Alix's elfin features took on a remarkably grim expression. '*He's* not expecting *me*. But I'm what he's going to get. I don't know if he'll be booking in under his own name. Shall I give you a description of him?'

'That would be most useful.' The woman paused. A warmth came into her eyes that was quite genuine, and very different from her professional manner. 'I think that if someone else were delivered to you by mistake, they would hardly complain! You remind me of her.' Natalie indicated the painting again. 'Some people have a certain natural flair for this. Perhaps, if you find you're not too tired by the end of the evening, you'd care to have a drink with me afterwards?'

Natalie had soft brown eyes, her skin was flawlessly clear, and the few laughter-lines at the corners of her eyes only accentuated her maturity and poise. The beautifully tailored burgundy velvet dress hinted at narrow hips, a waist not yet thickened, and a small and shapely bust. She seemed fine-boned and elegant, like valuable china. Alix's stomach flipped at the sudden and involuntary thought, *What would she look like, down on those elegant knees?*

'The role of a slave can be quite entrancing.' Natalie spoke as if she could read Alix's thought. 'Tonight, though, you shall be mistress. Allow me to show you to your dressing-room. We can attire you fully, if you wish.'

Alix held Natalie's gaze, reached down without looking, and tugged the sash of her summer raincoat. The front fell open.

From hips to breasts her body was laced tightly into a black leather basque. She knew her bare flesh above the basque top gleamed in the soft lighting of the corridor where the stiff leather forced her breasts up into half-moons. Her long legs were laced into skin-tight glove-leather trousers, the legs thonged down the outside. Below that, ankle boots with three-inch heels encased her feet.

At her belt she had hung a short-handled, thonged whip, much like the one in the painting.

'Well,' Alix said, 'how's that?'

'Impromptu, but perfect,' the older woman breathed. She was no longer *grande dame*, her brown eyes fixed on Alix in unsmiling lust. 'There

93

are some additional toys in the dressing-room that you may wish to consider, that is all.'

Behind them, at the front door, a discreet bell chimed. Alix looked thoughtfully towards the front of the house. She did not close her coat.

'Our guests prefer to be private upon entering and leaving,' Natalie said. 'I'm sure you'll understand, my dear. Oh – and what name do you wish to be known by here?'

'Vixen.' Alix blinked, thinking, Where did *that* come from? But, hey, I kind of like it.

'In that case, Mistress Vixen, the maid will show you to your room.' Natalie leaned over to what Alix had taken to be an ornamental telephone table and now saw it had tiny closed-circuit TV screens fitted. One showed a view of the street and the steps leading up to the door.

A dark-haired man stood on the step, gazing uncomfortably up and down the street and shifting from foot to foot. As he turned, Alix got a glimpse of his face. She found her lips curving in a very nasty smile. 'Yep. That's him . . .'

'Mistress Vixen?'

'That's my "friend".' Alix looked at Natalie. 'You did say it could be involuntary. Can you *make* him come to me?'

'Of course. We do this all the time.' Natalie briskly rang a concealed bell. A small girl with dark curly hair, wearing a tiny black dress and lacy white apron, walked into the lobby. 'Your maid, Chantelle. Please retire now. Chantelle will show you a monitor – you may watch your friend.'

Alix nodded. She hardly noticed the route by which the little maid led her into the mansion, through pale gold corridors and a succession of tall doors. Within a few moments Chantelle swung open a door that was thickly padded on the inside and ushered her into a room. It held a dressing-table and mirror, and four immense wardrobes.

'Here! You can watch!' The little French girl leaned over the dressing-table to flick the switch on a mini-monitor. Her short black skirt rode up. She wore lacy black stockings and a black lace garter-belt, tight enough for the pale flesh of her thighs and buttocks to be forced proudly up as she bent over.

Alix's hand moved, accidentally knocking against something hanging from her belt. It was the hard black leather handle of the whip, bought in Soho a few hours earlier.

The maid looked over her shoulder without straightening up. Her pert breasts were thrust forward under the skimpy covering of her bodice. 'I didn't call you "Mistress", Mistress Vixen. Are you going to punish me?'

I know how to do this, Alix thought, exhilarated. I know how to enjoy doing this. The fluttering in her stomach intensified.

'No,' Alix said silkily. 'I *may* punish you before the evening ends. Or I may not. It depends.'

Alix put one hand on the girl's plump rump and pushed her sharply aside. She seated herself at the dressing-table. The monitor's tiny picture was in colour, and well-defined; she could see every detail of the lobby, and of Natalie. The viewpoint looked down from above. The security camera was obviously hidden in one of the plaster wreathes on the ceiling.

The street door closed. A man in a dark shell-suit jacket and boots stepped inside the lobby. His outstretched hand pushed a silver-and-black card towards Natalie. Alix fiddled with a knob on the monitor and brought the sound up.

'But I was invited!' the man's deep voice protested. It was Vince Russell, all right.

Natalie's voice came calm and chilly through the speaker. 'I'm afraid there are a number of forged invitations in circulation. This is one of them. Besides, I hardly think you can be a guest of one of our most distinguished patrons.'

Her glance swept him from head to foot. Vince had obviously attempted to dress up for the occasion. The black track suit and T-shirt had been replaced by chinos and a shirt. They didn't conceal his muscular frame, or make it look any smarter. Alix realised that he knew it too; she could tell by the way he kept glancing around, and how he tensed his big muscular shoulders.

Good . . .

'I'm here because I was invited,' Vince growled. He scratched at his close-cropped head. 'Get used to the idea, woman. I've got a pretty good idea what goes on here. I think I'm going to enjoy giving one of you bitches what you've got coming to you.'

'You've got it coming to *you*, Vince' Alix whispered, leaning forward, intent on the tiny image.

'You wouldn't want me to go to the authorities.' Vince Russell smiled arrogantly. 'Let's not fuck about. I want one of your girls, and I want her now.'

'I don't think so.' Natalie's tone was icy. '*Stewards!*'

Two men stepped out of an anteroom beside the front door, its entrance completely concealed. Both were big, with the muscles of weight-lifters. Both wore nothing except tight black leather G-strings, and weight-lifters' leather belts strapped around their thick waists. Cuffs hung from the belts. Their oiled skin glistened in the corridor's dim light.

'Okay, okay – I'm going. I can take a hint,' Vince Russell snarled, and attempted to elbow between the two men to open the mansion's front door.

Instantly, before he could act, each steward grabbed one of his arms and swept his legs out from under him with a kick. Vince hit the carpet face-down, hard. The taller steward dropped to his knees – smack in the centre of Vince's back.

Alix gasped.

So quick that Alix hardly saw it, the bigger steward whipped a pair of handcuffs off his belt and neatly cuffed Vince's wrists behind his back. Then he stood up. With one bare, hard, muscular foot, he kicked Vince's legs apart. Natalie walked forward and placed her low-heeled shoe on Vince's groin. Vince Russell froze.

As she watched the monitor, Alix's hand slipped down between her leather-clad legs. She rubbed at the crotch-seam, pushing it into her hot flesh, naked underneath.

'Mistress Vixen . . .' The French maid leaned over the dressing-table. Her small round breasts pressed into Alix's bare shoulder. 'Permit me to pleasure you, Mistress. Please!'

Alix reached up and wound her fingers in the girl's dark hair. 'Do it!'

The maid's hands slid down to the waistband of Alix's tight black leather jeans. Her fingers undid the button and slid down the zip. Alix raised her hips in the chair so that the girl could slide the trousers down over her buttocks, dragging them down to her knees. Quickly, the girl knelt between

Alix's legs. Alix saw her head dip forward. She returned her attention to the screen.

'You can't do this to me!' Vince Russell yelled.

'Can't I?' Natalie ground her heel firmly into the supine man's crotch. 'I think I can . . .'

Slender fingers stroked Alix's thighs. A fingertip pushed its way into the fine hair of her pubic mound. Alix, without looking down, said, 'Don't keep me waiting!'

'No, Mistress!'

A hot wet tongue jabbed Alix's clitoris. She held herself rigid in the chair. The tongue dipped, swirled, and pushed into her hot cleft, stabbing in a hard rhythm.

On screen, Natalie turned her back on the sprawled body of Vince Russell. The big man lay flat on his back, legs apart, gazing up at the muscular stewards with bewilderment and fury on his face.

'I'll have Howard on you!' he raged, lifting his head to shout at the soignée older woman. 'You bitch, I'll see you in the street! You can't *do* this to me!'

Pulses of pleasure shot through Alix's sex. Little orgasms thrilled through her flesh, building and subsiding, responding to the girl's expert and determined tongue. Alix stared at the camera view – straight down between Vince's spread legs.

A faint bulge was pressing at the front of his trousers.

Alix leaned forward, staring intently. One of the stewards put his foot on Vince's shoulder and pushed him back on the floor, pinning him there. Vince's hips moved, squirming. His arousal was unmistakable now.

Oh yeah . . . !' Alix grinned in triumphant amazement. Her body flushed, pleasure peaking in her sex. 'Oh *yeah* . . . yes! *Yes!*'

As an undeniable erection poked out the cloth of Vince's trouser-fly, the French maid's tongue thrust deep into Alix's wet sex and brought her to climax. Alix's buttocks left the seat of the chair, her face contorted as she squeezed a last throb of pleasure from her flesh.

The maid's sweating face dropped down against Alix's leg. Her hot breath feathered Alix's skin. 'Was that satisfactory, Mistress Vixen?'

'*Yeah* . . . I mean, yes.' Alix recovered her composure. 'It was okay, I guess.'

The maid grinned.

The monitor showed the lobby still, in which Natalie and the stewards all stared at Vince Russell's bulging trousers. Vince's face reddened as Alix watched. He jerked his shoulders, trying to get his cuffed hands out from behind his back. The steel held him immobile. He brought his legs together and his knees up, trying to hide his arousal. His face was red as fire.

'Well, well,' Natalie said, her expression thoughtful.

Alix squirmed on her seat, unable to suppress a giggle. She yanked up her leather jeans and fastened them, not taking her eyes off the screen.

'It seems you're here for a reason,' the elegant woman said. 'You are a foul-mouthed low-life, Mr Russell. I can't do anything about that. I can, however, deal with your behaviour here as I see fit. You are going to be punished for your bad manners. You are going to be punished until you are truly, truly sorry.'

The big man's body lay utterly still on the carpet, hands still cuffed behind him, his expression strained. Alix leaned closer to the monitor.

'You called us "bitches",' Natalie continued, stepping closer until she stared down at Vince Russell. 'I don't think you know what a bitch is. I don't think you've ever met one. But you will. You'll meet one in just a moment. I'm going to give you to Mistress Vixen. And she will teach you never to show disrespect again.'

'No! You can't do this!' His close-cropped head lifted a little off the carpet. He gazed up at her, open-mouthed. The seams of the shell-suit split across the shoulders as he wrenched his arms. It did no good. The cuffs still held him. Vince shouted, 'I don't want that! You know I don't! Let me out of here, or I'll call the police!'

The immaculate woman stared down at Vince Russell. His erection strained at his trousers. He lay before her, helpless to conceal it.

'You're going to be humiliated,' Natalie said slowly, 'until you can't stand any more. We're going to punish you, Mr Russell. We're going to punish you—' her voice whip-cracked '—*until you can't stand.*'

Vince Russell's hips jerked.

His body slumped back on the carpet.

A dark wet stain began to spread over the fly of his trousers.

'He came in his pants,' Alix whispered, delighted. 'He came in his pants, in front of her.'

'Don't think that will save you,' Natalie's voice crackled harsh through the monitor speaker. 'There's plenty more in you yet. And I know just the mistress to get it out of you. Stewards! Take him to Mistress Vixen.'

'No!' he yelled. 'No, wait, *no*—!'

The oiled, muscular men grabbed him under the armpits and dragged him down the corridor, out of the camera's range. The French maid leaned across Alix and switched off the monitor.

'Mistress will need to get ready,' she breathed. The pupils of her dark eyes dilated. 'You may use anything that is here, Mistress.'

Without waiting for an answer, she walked across the room and began to fling open the doors of the wardrobes. Alix sat still for a moment until her breathing subsided. *Where are they taking him, what will they do to him?*

A knock on the door announced Natalie. The woman smiled, her soft breasts still rising and falling a little rapidly under the burgundy-coloured dress. 'Chantelle, dear, I've put him in room seven. Please show Mistress Vixen there when she's ready. It won't harm him to anticipate.'

Alix frowned. 'Are you sure this is a good idea? I mean, I wouldn't want this place to get into trouble.'

Natalie's laughter chimed. She smoothed her velvet gown down over her hips, glancing at her feet. 'What a shame I wasn't wearing higher heels. I so seldom engage myself these days, I've quite lost the habit . . . Mistress Vixen, you are not under the impression that your friend genuinely thinks himself a prisoner?'

'I . . . don't know.'

'You will recall, he *has* been informed of what goes on at *Pleasure Bound*.' Natalie absently reached out and tugged the French maid's bodice down another half-inch. Dark-haired Chantelle

101

giggled. Natalie continued. 'And he's an interesting man, your Mr Russell. I think he's seen genuine violence. I *don't* think he is one of those people who becomes aroused by that. I think that the minute he saw Richie and Jan in their costumes, he knew exactly what was going on. Whether he liked the idea or not is another matter! He may protest that he does not wish to be humiliated.' Her eyes gleamed, and in her cut-glass accent she added, 'Whether he says he likes it or not, his cock went up like a flag-pole!'

Alix nodded. 'Yeah. Like a rock. But he was *blushing*!'

'I will tell you something else.' The older woman touched an elegant finger to her lip. 'I can tell – he has never done this before. He has never been a slave, or a master. But now, for tonight, he is *your* slave. To punish however you wish. Whether he wants you to, or not. He cannot stop you now.'

'Oh, I'll punish Vince, all right,' Alix said grimly. 'Trust me.'

She picked up a pair of elbow-length leather gloves, holding out her arms for Natalie to lace them up. Chantelle, in her maid's costume, went busily to and fro from the wardrobes. Alix saw a glitter of steel and leather in the dark interiors. She could not quite make out what it was that Chantelle was laying out for her inspection. Black glove-leather, with two almond-shaped holes . . .

A mask, Alix realised. A mask that would cover her entire head, make her faceless, anonymous, unknowable, aloof. She picked up the soft leather garment. From the assorted instruments, she picked up a thick-handled black riding-crop. 'This'll be fine. Okay, let's do it.'

Natalie opened the dressing-room door. 'Chantelle will show you the way.'

Alix strode out of the door and down the corridor, following the maid's pert bottom. The heels of her boots thunked against the carpet. The leather jeans clung tightly to her skin, and the laced bodice constricted her torso, making her walk with an upright stance.

'Here.' The maid indicated a door.

Alix handed the silk-lined leather mask to Chantelle. 'I want him to see exactly who it is, first . . .'

She opened the door and stepped into the room beyond.

The room was windowless, painted all matt-black, light coming from invisible sources. Her eyes swept across the ring-bolts fastened to the walls and set into the floor. Apart from a solid oak chair, also bolted to the floor, and a padded object like a gym horse, the room was empty of equipment.

The two stewards stood holding Vince Russell between them. As she shut the door, they simultaneously bowed their heads and murmured, 'Mistress Vixen . . .'

The big man, cuffed and pinned between them, raised his head. His eyes widened. '*You!*'

'Me. Your little gym student . . .' Alix stopped, fists on leather-clad hips, beside the stewards. She nodded at the leather briefs and belts they wore. 'You have more of those?'

'Yes, Mistress.'

'Strip him. Put him in them.'

'You can't do this!' Vince Russell bellowed. 'Look, girl – whatever your name is – the bet's off, I give in, I quit, I'm not doing this!'

His face flushed red. Sweat glistened in his cropped hair. Alix let her icy, supercilious gaze travel down to the naked male chest visible between the buttons of his ripped shirt, to the wet blotch at the junction of his thighs. Vince followed her gaze. He coloured a vivid scarlet.

My God, he *is* blushing!

Alix stepped closer and brought the riding-crop up between his thighs, just touching the crotch of his trousers. She raised her eyes to meet Vince Russell's humiliated gaze.

Without looking at the stewards, she snarled harshly, 'I said strip him! I *don't* want to have to say it twice.'

'Okay. Fair enough.' Vince shrugged, as best he could in handcuffs. 'You've got your own back for the gym. Now tell them to let me go. I'm *warning* you—!'

Alix stepped back as the two men grabbed him. The larger of the two ripped his shirt open to the waist. The smaller, dark steward knelt, grabbed Vince Russell's trousers and tore them down.

The big man swore, thrashed, and made an apparently genuine effort to punch, kick, and bite his way free – to no avail. Cuffs were removed, his clothes stripped, and cuffs snapped back, with a speed that left Alix breathless. She stood tapping the crop against her leather-clad thigh until they had finished, and Vince Russell was held before her, naked but for tight black leather briefs.

His cock was stuffed and buckled into a leather crotch-piece, with a strap that could be tightened as she might desire. When they turned him round for her inspection, she saw that the back of the briefs were cut away, so that his white buttocks were forced painfully up and out of the leather.

'You won't get away with this!' Vince blustered, straining to look over his broad, naked shoulder.

Alix surveyed him. Seconds ticked past. A muscle jumped in his thigh, below where the tight leather cut in. His buttocks clenched. He was trying not to move his body, she saw – and he was trying to keep from looking at the padded leather and wood stand. She walked around to the front of him. His leather crotch-piece was bulging.

Vince Russell's fascinated gaze shifted, only to encounter her riding-crop, tapping gently against her black-gloved hand. 'Don't you dare touch me, you bitch! I'll have you for assault!'

Alix smiled. 'But I'll have had you first.'

At her nod, the larger steward pushed Vince Russell face-forward across the wooden horse. It was high enough to catch him in the upper belly. Breath whooshed out of his lungs. As he lay winded, both stewards cuffed his wrists and ankles to ring-bolts on the floor, and stood back.

'You can go,' Alix ordered.

'Yes, Mistress Vixen!'

The door closed behind them. Alix walked slowly, completely around Vince Russell where he sprawled, face-down and chained. The wooden horse was high enough that he had to strain on tiptoe, and the leather padding still pressed hard into his groin.

Alix looked at his jutting bare cheeks.

'You look chilly,' she purred. 'Shame you can't get any exercise. I'll warm you up, shall I?'

The big man twisted his head around, staring up at her furiously. Sweat ran down his face. His eyes were a soft brown, she saw, and held a badly

105

concealed panic. He licked his lips. The straining muscles of his thighs could not shift his bum an inch away from her. Tendons in his throat jutted. Scarlet-faced, he bawled, 'Fuck off, bitch!'

Alix walked around until she stood behind him, where he could not turn to see her. 'That's no language – for a slave.'

His cock, crushed under his body and strapped in leather, swelled impressively.

'You're going to learn,' she said. She reached out and put the very tip of the crop between his spread legs, resting it on his tight briefs where they covered his scrotum. 'You're going to learn to call me "Mistress".'

His body froze.

So quietly that she hardly heard him, he whispered, 'Let me go.'

Alix drew her arm back. 'Maybe. Maybe not.'

'Please.' His sweat-soaked head lifted, although he could only stare ahead, and he spoke into empty air. 'I'm sorry about— Make them let me out of here!'

'Oh. You're sorry.' Alix brought the crop down – hard. The wicked thin leather lashed down across both his bare cheeks, where they were forced up, skin taut. His body leaped, helplessly, held down by the cuffs.

Vince Russell yelled. '*Fuck!* Jesus, no! You stupid bitch, get me out of here!'

Alix watched a thin red stripe of inflamed flesh glow across Vince Russell's backside.

'Only my friends call me "bitch",' she said. 'You can call me "Mistress Vixen". And you will. Like the lady said, I'm going to teach you manners.'

'You fucking—'

Alix lifted the crop and lashed him, harder, a dozen times, laying red weals alternately across each buttock.

'*No!*' The big man sobbed with frustration. 'You ain't going to teach me nothing, there's nothing you can teach me! Oh, please, girl!'

'There's plenty I can teach you,' Alix said. 'You're doing well. But I'm going to teach you to do it properly.'

The man made a noise between a swear word and a sob. He raised his head, his dripping eyes bright. 'Do what you like. It doesn't *matter. Babes!* has lost this bet.'

'What?' Alix could only stare, completely taken aback. 'Oh. Oh, yeah. The *bet.*'

'I'm no slave,' Vince Russell growled. 'I'm a *man*. I should have been a Master here – then I'd have won the bet. This doesn't turn me on at all. You *lose*, girl.'

Alix stared at him. 'Do I?'

She walked around behind Vince Russell. His naked buttocks glowed red, striped with a dozen weals on each hind cheek. Alix shifted the riding crop to her left hand. She cupped her gloved right hand and brought it up between his legs, grabbing his leather-bound crotch. His whole body jerked. He could not pull away from her hand.

Gently, she laid the crop across his bare bum.

Through the thin leather she felt his nuts tighten in his scrotum. His massive hard-on strained against the leather cut-away briefs. His sweating body writhed. He groaned.

Alix, unseen by Vince Russell, smiled. '*I* think my slave is turned on. Now. Like I said. I'm going to teach you to beg . . .'

107

Chapter Eight

AIR-CONDITIONING HUMMED in the *Babes!* editor's office, making it pleasantly cool despite the morning heat-wave outside in Canary Wharf.

Richard Stanley came in at eight, chatting to one of the photo-models for a few minutes before he entered his office. She was a big woman (*November* being a specialist month), and her cleavage caused him to make an entirely specious excuse about needing further biographical details so that he could stand there and talk with her a little longer.

Sometimes this job *is* all it's cracked up to be, he thought cheerfully, slinging his briefcase onto his desk. Then, when he had powered up and checked his e-mail messages for 22 August, his expression turned to a frown. *And sometimes it's shit*.

He thumbed the intercom. 'Get Vince Russell up to my office. *Now.*'

Thirty minutes passed.

Richard Stanley sat behind his desk, jacket off, red braces bright against his ivory shirt with its rolled-up sleeves. He did not look up when he heard the knock on the door. 'Enter!'

He continued to tap at the keyboard for a full

minute before he deigned to raise his head.

Vince Russell stood in front of his desk. On duty as usual, the big man wore the building's brown security uniform. With his short hair, he looked even more of an ex-squaddie.

'Shut the door behind you. What do you *mean*, you lost the bet?' Richard demanded. He did not invite Russell to sit. 'Are you telling me you didn't go through with it?'

Vince Russell shifted from foot to foot, uncomfortably. He did not look directly at him, Richard noted. The man's gaze fixed on a point over Richard's left shoulder.

'Well?' Richard barked.

'No, sir.' Vince Russell's brown eyes sought Richard's face. Despite his upright stance, there was a hint of panic in his expression.

' "No" you did it, or "no" you didn't do it?'

'I went through with the bet, sir.'

'Then what's the problem?' Richard called up the new video file again on his monitor. The on-screen picture had sharp definition. He glanced up again, and caught Vince trying to stare around the edge of the monitor.

Russell looked sharply away as Richard saw him, returning to eyes-front. 'The bet wasn't whether someone would *do* it, sir. It was about whether it would be – enjoyable. It wasn't.'

'I see . . .' Richard lounged back in his chair. He reached for his cup and took a sip of aromatic coffee. The hot china cup stung his fingers. 'I see . . . You failed to find it at all arousing?'

'Failed completely, sir. Sorry.'

A bright summer morning sparkled through the office windows. Gulls soared over the river, white wings flashing. The same sun illuminated the rows of framed *Babes!* covers on the office walls. Apart from that and his workstation, the large office was empty. Richard preferred to keep it that way and remind people of the amount of floor-space he commanded.

'You're lying,' he said.

Taking his time, he looked back at Vince Russell standing on the white rug. A hint of pink flush showed under the shaved scalp stubble. Russell stared determinedly past Richard.

'Edmund Howard forwarded me a videotape this morning. From *Pleasure Bound.*' Richard enunciated the name very clearly. With a powerful twist, he swung the monitor around so that the other man was staring straight at it. 'I found it very interesting viewing.'

The video showed a black-walled room and a close-up of a big crop-haired man, unmistakably Vince Russell. His body was bent forward over a padded leather stand, his wrists handcuffed to ring-bolts in the floor. The shot just showed that his ankles were similarly shackled. A thick harness of leather straps was buckled around his naked chest, and the tight strap of a leather jock-strap forced his naked buttocks apart, tightly jerked up into his crotch. Although he struggled, he could do no more than shift his torso an inch or so either way.

Vince Russell stared at Richard, appalled.

On screen a masked figure clad head-to-foot in skin-tight black leather stood behind the helpless man. The woman – it was unmistakably a female figure – raised a black riding crop in her hand.

Richard keyed freeze-frame.

'It's *lies*!' Vince Russell roared. His fist slammed down on the desk. Richard barely stopped himself visibly startling. 'It's all bloody lies, whatever that fucking girl Alix says, whatever that bloody Madam shows you! It's lies! It might have *happened* – but the only one who knows how I *felt* is me, and I hated the whole fucking thing!'

Richard made his stare glacial.

Slowly, awkwardly, Vince Russell straightened up. His arms hung at his sides, his hands still knotted into fists. He gave a quick glance at the office door, as if afraid some PA might come charging in. He didn't look at Richard. A slow, heated flush rose, darkening his cheeks. 'Bloody lies, sir. Sorry. But it is. Sorry to let you down, but we *lost* that one.'

Richard let the atmosphere drop a few more degrees. He clasped his fingers lightly on the desk in front of him and let his gaze travel from the big man's flushed face, down to his boots, and back up again.

'Would you really like me to play you the video soundtrack?' he asked quietly. 'Would you, Vince? I think it might indicate that you're being less than honest with me. I don't like that. I don't think Mr Howard would like it, either. I'm certain my staff wouldn't like it, if they understood you were about to lose them their jobs because you won't tell the truth.'

'It has a soundtrack?' Russell's voice squeaked. He coughed. In a gruff tone, he added, 'Dubbed. Got to be. It wasn't me, sir.'

'You don't know what it says.'

'I don't care what it says, it wasn't me!'

Richard shot a sharp glance up at Russell's face.

111

He crossed one leg casually over the other, trouser-cuff pulling up to show an inch of red silk sock. With great deliberation, he smiled at Vince Russell.

'Alix Neville had you stripped.'

Vince Russell squinted rigidly, painfully ahead, out of the bright windows. The flush darkened his face still further. He licked his lips. 'Yes, sir.'

'Alix Neville whipped you.'

'Sir.' The big man began to sweat, tiny clear globules of moisture plainly visible on his brow.

'Did you hate it, Vincent?' Richard asked softly. He gazed at the big man's crotch. A slight bulge pressed against the uniform trousers.

'Yes . . .' It was an agonised protest. Russell's eyes strayed to the monitor, as if fascinated despite himself.

'Did you hate it when she tied you over that thing, and whipped your ass?'

Vince Russell looked helplessly around the room. He didn't meet Richard's eye. There was a definite bulge in his pants now. 'Of course I hated it!'

'So it wasn't you who begged her – *begged* her to carry on?'

'No!' Vince Russell put his feet apart at parade-rest and clasped his hands in front of him. He could not hide the erection jutting in his uniform trousers. He very slightly squirmed in his pants. His face was red as fire. 'I did not!'

'I think you did. Would you like to hear yourself beg?' Richard poised a finger over the keyboard. The big man shot him a look of mute appeal. Richard stared at Russell's stiff cock. He caught himself thinking, *If he moves, he'll come in his pants, right here in front of me*. Not normally attracted to men, Richard Stanley nonetheless found, as he watched the broad, sweating, muscled body of the ex-soldier, that his own rod stirred in his trousers at the thought.

What am I *doing*? Richard leaned forward, to be sure that his desk hid him from the waist down. I'm not meant to be having fun here. This is my job I'm worried about . . .

'I think you won the bet, Vince,' Richard said calmly. 'I think you got a great deal of gratification out of being given a damn good thrashing. And you're going to admit it. I don't care how humiliating you find it that you got off on being a slave, you're going to admit it publicly. Here, to me. And upstairs, to Edmund Howard. I'm not losing *Babes!* because you don't want to admit you liked being had by a beautiful woman wearing leather!'

The big man flushed bright crimson. He stared down at his boots. In an almost inaudible voice, he muttered, 'Yes.'

'Yes, what?'

Vince Russell's long-lashed brown eyes sought Richard's face. He mumbled, 'Yes. I wanted her to whip me. I – begged.'

Slowly Richard drew back his hand from the workstation keyboard. 'And you won the bet.'

The big man shifted his stance. His cock stood rock-hard in his pants. In an even lower tone, Vince Russell whispered, 'Yes. I won the bet, too.'

'So we're even with *Femme*. Good. You can go now.'

Richard turned back to his work. After a second, and without looking up, he snapped, 'I said, you can go! I'll have you sent up to Mr Howard when I need to.'

'Sir.' The man's voice sounded strangled.

Without raising his head, Richard covertly watched Vince Russell turn and walk towards the office door. The big man took two cautious steps, then stopped. A shudder passed through his whole body. Richard saw him grab the door-frame for support.

'Get out,' he snarled.

Vince Russell reached down, turned the door handle and let himself out; walking stiffly, gingerly, with his legs apart.

Richard's eyes glazed over. Then, shaking himself out of it, he pressed the key for his PA.

'Confirm my flight out to LA today,' he ordered briskly. 'Check the hotel booking. Arrange an interview for Vince Russell with Mr Howard. If anything comes down from upstairs while I'm at our West Coast offices, contact me immediately.'

The midday business flight out of Heathrow to LAX became an eighteen-hour grind. Richard Stanley leaned back in his seat in the first-class compartment. Half his mind was on Midnight Rose International's West Coast office. He tapped occasionally at the keys of his notebook computer.

He barely smiled at the blonde stewardess bringing him his drink. She's a dog, he thought, disappointed. Well, no, not a *dog*, exactly – but you do expect these girls to be a wee bit special.

Richard pushed up the window shade and stared out, giving up on the sales graphs. An endless blue sky held the plane like an insect, motionless in amber sunlight. The subsonic thrum of the airframe vibrated through his body. The sensation brought him to the edge of arousal. He crossed his legs. Outside, a frozen, oxygenless atmosphere. Inside, warmth and the soft throbbing of the engines. He listened to classical music on his headphones and sipped at his brandy, savouring the smooth bite.

I wonder what Vince or that girl are doing right now?

The intrusive thought made him suddenly aware of the silk shirt and light summer suit he was wearing. He ran a finger round under his collar. Warmth stirred in his groin. He imagined the masked girl on the CCTV footage, bringing the riding crop down across Vince Russell's naked buttocks . . .

What am *I* getting out of this? Richard thought, suddenly angry. Damn Vince Russell; I've never had any trouble pulling birds! I'm as adventurous as the next man!

But going clubbing or to the wine bars in the City isn't the same as picking up a total stranger for wild sex. Is it?

The seat-belt light pinged. He absently strapped himself in. The stewardess leaned across him to check the tautness of the belt. Her breast in its crisp white cotton shirt passed within inches of his face. Richard Stanley ignored her, frowning, his eyes narrowing as he thought.

Suppose I made a little bet with myself? And then informed Mr Howard of my success – with appropriate evidence, of course. *That* would put *Babes!* one up. That's going to put me ahead of *Femme* and no mistake.

The plane's nose dipped. His stomach dipped with it, G-force pressuring his body. The airframe juddered. Richard Stanley looked out of the window as the plane began its descent.

A brown haze hung over LA, only the Hollywood Hills pushing up out of it, green and breezy. The Pacific Ocean shone blue under a still-daytime sky. He rubbed at his eyes and leaned back with a show of casual inattention as they came in to land.

Not the blonde, he mused. I need a challenge. Something to really *impress* the MD . . .

LAX seethed, crowded. Humid air settled instantly around his skin in a film of sweat. He made it through Customs to the taxis outside and hastily put on his RayBans, blotting out the glare of the sky. Eighteen hours of sunshine. His body felt lagged. He stared into the brown-edged haze around the airport buildings, his lungs feeling as if he were breathing burning tyres.

The air-conditioning of the taxi was welcoming and cool as he settled back and gave the name of his hotel. His internal clock made this afternoon the early hours of the morning. He leaned back against the upholstery, the smell of leather pungent in his nostrils. Sleepily he gazed at the endless succession of two-storey detached houses and palm trees, the blocks of K-Marts and video stores, only rousing himself to check in to the hotel.

Once in his room, Richard Stanley stripped off his light business suit and shirt. He paced across the carpet, naked and barefoot, his skin tingling with the air-conditioning turned up high. The floor-length plate-glass window overlooked the internal courtyard of the hotel from the seventh storey. He gazed down at a startlingly blue swimming pool and Jacuzzis nestling in Astroturf under real palm trees.

A big-haired woman with a mahogany tan and a

116

buttercup-yellow bikini padded across the pool-surround and dived in. Moving water sent ripples of light across her strongly stroking body. She emerged on the near side of the pool, water sleeking her hair down flat, runnelling over her brown shoulders and between the swelling mounds of her breasts. She walked slowly up the pool steps. Glistening water shone on her flat stomach and dripped down from her yellow bikini-bottom, streaking her long, lean legs until the moisture dried in the hot sun.

Yeah . . . Richard Stanley murmured aloud, 'LA, here I come . . .'

Dusk came faster than he was used to in England. By the time he had phoned in to say he had arrived, eaten a light snack and put on his robe, the evening sky was turning royal blue. He found his way down to the pool deck, nonetheless, and padded out into the courtyard.

Hidden lights glowed in the trees surrounding the hot tubs. Warm shadows hid the rising hotel walls, interrupted only by one or two room-lights. Richard cast a brief glance at the pool. Two or three women were swimming and calling to each other, obviously together. An older couple rested at one edge, by the pool steps, treading water and talking quietly.

Close by, one of the hot tubs bubbled and steamed. Wisps of whiteness drifted up into the evening air. A single figure occupied the tub.

A woman, Richard saw – a young woman, regular features, tanned, her gold-blonde hair fastened up on the crown of her head. Under the shimmering, boiling surface of the water, Richard glimpsed

117

a buttercup-yellow bikini. The roiling surface of the Jacuzzi hid most of her body, but her tanned shoulders were shapely.

Her eyes were closed. Richard studied her incredibly long golden lashes for a moment. As if she felt his gaze, she opened her eyes. A clear blue stare surveyed him for a second before she lowered her gaze.

Richard Stanley moved in under the shadow of the trees. He dropped his white cotton towelling robe on a chair. He stood for a moment to show off his muscled body in his tight black swimming trunks – the work-outs really paid off.

'Mind if I join you?' he murmured, doing his best to sound like an English Hollywood star.

The blonde woman's gaze went beyond him. A smile spread across her generous mouth. Her blue eyes twinkled.

'Maybe,' she said, her voice Southern and soft, 'maybe you should ask my girlfriend . . . Hi, Jade, honey.'

Richard turned his head. A tall, slender, muscled African-American woman padded across the pool surround. Her black hair was bound back in corn-rows, the end of each narrow braid jingling with a metal bead. Her legs scissored, long, smooth-skinned and velvety-brown, her one-piece black swimsuit, cut high at the thigh, disclosing smooth narrow hips, barely hiding taut, round breasts.

'Oh.' Richard became aware that he was staring.

The African-American woman swept past him. Her cornrow braids jingled again as she bent over from the waist, over the hot tub, narrow brown buttocks barely covered by her swimsuit. Sweat broke out on his forehead. The front of his swimming trunks filled as his cock began to swell.

The woman, Jade, continued to lean down until she could plant a kiss smack on the open mouth of the blonde woman in the hot tub. Their tongues entwined wetly.

'Sorry,' Jade lifted her head and said throatily, without looking round. 'This is a *private* tub now; d'ya mind?'

The blonde woman in the tub hitched her body up onto the tub seat, below the surface. It brought her big, rounded breasts above the bubbling water. Droplets of water streamed down over her tanned, glistening skin.

'But—' he said.

She smiled at him, staring at the area of his groin. His trunks did not conceal his arousal. His cock strained the stretchy cloth forward, pulling the waistband of his trunks slightly open.

'Sorry, honey,' she breathed, 'but you ain't got nothing that we need . . .'

As the African-American woman's brown body slid into the hot tub beside her, the blonde woman put a wet arm around her waist. She kissed the other woman on the lips. Her free hand vanished under the surface of the Jacuzzi's steaming water.

Richard Stanley turned and limped, slowly and awkwardly, to where he had left his white towelling gown. He put it on.

When he could move comfortably, he went to the pool and swam thirty lengths. He was still swimming when the pool deck closed for the night.

Richard assumed that when the office shake-up was done, his West Coast colleagues would have laid on some night-life entertainment. He never got the chance to find out. He fell asleep in a meeting around three in the afternoon.

'I have some documents to check back at the hotel,' he lied, rubbing his eyes as if he were thoughtful. He stood up from the boardroom table. His mouth tasted stale. 'Let's reconvene first thing tomorrow, okay?'

'Six a.m., sharp.' Nick Laurie, his tall, redheaded American counterpart, grinned cheerfully. 'I guess you don't want to waste any of Mr Howard's time, huh?'

Up, Richard thought, confident of the idiom, *your smug ass. Oh, my head* . . .

He took a taxi back to his hotel. Inside, he reached up and tugged the knot of his tie loose and undid the top button of his shirt. The jet-lag's going, he thought hopefully. It won't do to be on less than top form tomorrow. There's always office politics, even this side of the Atlantic . . .

Richard shifted on the seat to look ahead. '*There.*' He pointed to the entrance to a shopping mall. 'Stop there, that's fine.'

A mall's bound to have a drugstore, he thought, paying off the cab-driver. I'll get a couple of packets of industrial-strength caffeine tablets. That'll set me right.

He fumbled through dollar bills, the welcome shadow of a palm tree falling across him. Sun blazed back whitely from the pavement. Acrid air caught in the back of his throat. He picked up his briefcase and walked smartly across the pedestrian precinct, pushing between the crowds of white, African-American and Asian-American families into the air-conditioned cool of the mall.

Sunlight gleamed clear through the polarised glass roof, robbed of its Pacific harshness. The shop-window displays in book shops and toy stores looked unexpectedly muted, not garish like British malls – tame, almost. Richard threaded his way between teenagers, small children, baby-buggies, couples walking hand in hand. He bought a stack of caffeine tablets in the drugstore and stopped by a vending machine to grab a Coke and swallow a handful of the pills.

That's better . . .

Richard looked up, realising he had stopped outside the *Victoria's Secret* store.

Demure bottle-green and burgundy satin bras, knickers and camisoles dressed the models in the window. Their plastic mannequin faces smiled aimlessly, no hint of seductiveness or eroticism.

Tame, Richard thought. *Tomorrow, I'll make* sure *Nick shows me where the action is.*

But it'd be better if I found it myself.

It's like this, Mr Howard, I don't think Neville or Russell should be asked to do anything I wouldn't do . . .

Especially if I do it better.

He walked towards the mall's main exit. Now that he was looking, a hundred beautiful women walked past the glittering windows: that one in the white crop-top, brown breasts bouncing as she ran after her friends; the blonde one in pink high heels with the neatest, tightest ass in the world; a redhead, scented with some exotic flowery perfume, who spilled her keys from her purse and bent over, giving him a view straight down her blue dress! . . .

So how *do I* . . .? Richard stepped onto the eleva-tor, briefcase in one hand, jacket over the other arm, gazing around. *You can't just go up to one and say, 'Get your kit off . . .'*

He stepped off onto the second floor. A restaurant dominated the far end. He turned the other way, walking between the rail of the central well and the successive shop windows. Fewer people browsed up here. Ahead, a group of three girls clustered around a dress-shop window display. He slowed down.

High-school girls – no, young women, eighteen or so. All three looked Japanese, long glossy black manes of hair flowing down their backs.

Richard slowed down still more.

One – she wore a white blouse and a sand-coloured cable-knit sweater over tiny brown velvet shorts – shot a glance at him and murmured something. Her body was slender, curving at hip and bust. Her long hair was held back from her smooth young face by a red Alice band. She giggled.

Behind her, one of her friends put both hands on the girl's shoulders and stood on tiptoe to peer over. This girl wore a red sweater and a tiny black mini-skirt, black tights, and a narrow-brimmed black felt hat pulled down to her little ears: that and her wide epicanthic black eyes made her look utterly elfin. She darted him a dazzling glance and said something behind her hand to the third girl, a taller young woman in a blue ra-ra skirt and white sailor-collared blouse, who swung a shiny red clutch-bag from one wrist.

This one's dark eyes raked him up and down.

I'm in luck!

'Hello.' Richard stopped and smiled. He wondered suddenly if they spoke only Japanese.

'Oh, you're *English*! Keiko, he's *English*!' the one

in sweater and shorts exclaimed. She put her hands behind her back, and swung one patent-shoed toe-tip side to side on the shiny floor tiles, staring down as if astonished at her temerity in speaking. Richard let his gaze slide up the length of her slim ankle, calf and thigh. Her smooth skin glowed amber through her fine pantyhose. She hung her head, not meeting his gaze; her long black lashes lowered but her lips curving into a smile.

Richard noted moisture as she licked her pink-lipsticked lower lip. A warmth began to make itself felt in his groin.

'Say something else! Please!' Keiko, it seemed, was the one with the hat. She skipped up and down on the spot in her excitement, her small breasts bouncing under her red sweater. Richard caught his breath. She wasn't wearing a bra.

'Yes, I'm English.' Richard heard his accent shift rapidly towards the cut-glass. 'And you 're from – where?'

'Oh, from *here*, *borrr*-ing!' the almond-eyed girl in the sailor-collared shirt said, in pure West Coast American. 'I'm Makiko. This is Yuri. And Keiko. Can we buy you a coffee or something? So we can, like, hear you talk and stuff?'

'Certainly. I'm flattered.' Richard smiled sexily at Makiko. His mind raced. Coffee in some mall diner, maybe. But with a bit more nerve . . . His mind furiously racing, his gaze fell on the shop window display they were standing next to. A dress shop – a pricey one, judging by the fact that it was almost deserted – with a row of mannequins in the window sporting evening dresses.

'I don't want to interrupt your shopping,' he

said.

Makiko's dark gaze fell. She was tall enough that Richard found himself gazing down the square neck of the sailor-blouse, at the swell of her amber breasts. 'Oh, like, we don't have enough credit to shop here! I *wish*.'

The other two girls nodded. Keiko adjusted her hat, the lifting of her arms bringing her short sweater up, showing an inch of bare tummy above the waistband of her skirt. She said wistfully, 'My allowance ran out.'

'Mine too.'

'And me!'

'Well.' Richard inclined his head. 'I hate to see ladies in distress. Before we have that coffee, allow me to take you shopping.'

'*Wheeee!*' Yuri grabbed his arm, her waist-length black hair flying. She reached up with one hand to adjust her red Alice band. Her other arm squeezed his forearm close to her body, against her skinny, warm torso and the softness of the side of what must be, under the blouse and sweater, a remarkably full, round breast.

'Yes!' Keiko exclaimed.

'Let's go!' Makiko seized his other arm. Between the two giggling girls, Richard found himself swept into the store; Keiko tiptoeing behind them. The heady scent of perfume and young female bodies filled his nostrils.

'We want to try, like, *everything*,' tall Makiko instructed the sales assistant as she came forward. 'Is that your changing cubicle? *Okay!*'

'We'll get dressed,' little Yuri said, 'and you can tell us what looks cool. I mean, like, a guy always knows, okay? And you're a guy, so . . .' Her black eyes twinkled.

'We forgot to ask his name,' Keiko whispered. She reached up and pulled her little velvet hat off, staring around the expensive store in awe. Her black gaze finished at Richard. Her cheeks blushed a faint, delicate rose. 'That is *so* uncool.'

'I'm Richard,' Richard said.

'Oh, wow.' Keiko's dark pupils dilated. She licked her pink lip again. 'I could listen to you, like, all *day*. Are you in the States for long?'

'I'm afraid not.'

Makiko murmured, 'Then we'll have to make the best of you while we've got you, huh, Richard? That is such a *cool* name!'

Richard felt both his elbows seized by her and Yuri, who whisked him into a seat in front of the curtained-off communal changing cubicles, next to a set of three full-length mirrors.

'This is so *exciting*!' Yuri bent forward, reached over her shoulders with both hands and pulled her sand-coloured sweater off over her head. She straightened up, cheeks flushed, long black hair in tangles, her eyes bright. Her white blouse was pulled half out of her shorts. She held out the sweater. 'Will you look after this for me?'

'Certainly.' The wool felt warm with her body-heat. Richard folded the garment over his lap, watching the tall slender Makiko direct the sales assistant with the efficiency of a drill-sergeant: whole racks of dresses were ferried into the communal changing-room.

He looked at little Yuri, still flushed, with her blouse disarranged. Under the rumpled cotton, Richard could see the outline of her bra-cup. 'I thought that all Japanese girls were demure . . .'

Yuri seated herself on the arm of his chair. She looked down at him with a small, shy smile. 'And, like, I thought English guys were all uptight? Like, you never think about girls?'

'Oh, I think about girls,' Richard said gravely. 'In fact, I think about them a lot.'

Yuri shot a look at the other two teenagers. Makiko abandoned the dress racks for a moment and came over, Keiko in her wake.

'For example,' he went on, 'I don't believe I've seen three girls quite as pretty as you in London. Not ever.'

They giggled behind their hands, their heads together, loose black hair flying. Keiko, in her little black mini-skirt, stood on tiptoe to whisper in Makiko's ear. The taller girl bit her lip, eyes sparkling, and took Yuri's hand. The little girl in the velvet shorts listened, put her fingers over her mouth, and nodded excitedly.

'Richard.' Makiko bent over him where he sat in the chair. He looked down the front of her sailor-blouse, at pert breasts in lacy white bra-cups. 'We decided. You can, like, watch us. But don't give us away!'

With that, all three of them whisked behind the cubicle curtain, and Richard was left alone. He glanced around the shop, once. No other customers. The mall outside looked quiet. One assistant, on the far side of the shop floor, leafed through a magazine . . .

He carefully put his jacket, his briefcase and Yuri's sweater down beside his chair.

As he straightened up, his eye caught movement in the nearest mirror. The cubicle curtain twitched slightly back. From where he sat, he couldn't see behind it. But in the mirror, he realised, he looked straight through to the inside of the changing-room.

Keiko faced the mirrored wall, her back to him. She pulled her red sweater over her head. A tiny pink bra-strap crossed her narrow back. Richard watched her undo the side of her black mini-skirt. The scrap of material dropped, snagging at her knees, and she wriggled her bum from side to side until her skirt fell to the floor, and she stepped out of it. A matching pink pair of bikini pants encased her tiny round buttocks.

Richard shifted in the depths of the upholstered chair. His cock began to swell. Unconsciously he reached down and hitched the crotch of his suit trousers away.

What am I doing—? He stared around.

On the far side of the shop, the assistant was still ignoring the world.

Richard put his hand back into his lap. He rubbed at his crotch, feeling himself become half erect. His gaze was riveted on the view in the mirror. Keiko peeled off her black pantyhose and turned around to choose one of the dresses. Her breasts were round and full in the fragile pink bra. He glimpsed a darkness at her crotch, pubic hair visible through the thin material of her panties. His cock jumped into his hand.

Yuri obscured his view of Keiko as she bent down to undo her shoes. She was naked. Her full, brown-tipped breasts hung free, jouncing as she fought a recalcitrant shoe-lace. As she straightened up, she glanced at the mirror and winked directly at Richard.

Yuri turned her back, hands on tiny hips, and

127

looked at him over her shoulder, posing.

'Oh God!' His rod stiffened painfully. Heat flushed the hard muscles of his thighs and his blood raced in his belly. He felt sweat darkening his shirt under his arms. He glanced hastily around the shop again. A fierce feeling of triumph coursed through him: wait until I tell them about this back at the office! Wait until I tell Mr Howard I've won a bet . . .

Makiko came into the mirror's view.

Richard looked over his shoulder. The shop assistant was walking towards a far door. As he watched, she vanished into the restroom.

He plunged his hand down the front of his pants. His fingers cupped the prickingly hot skin of his scrotum, gently squeezing his balls. His cock thickened and speared upwards. In the glass, he watched Makiko unbutton her sailor-blouse and pull it off. Her plain white cotton bra enclosed a pair of beautifully rounded breasts. She was aware of his gaze. The thin cotton poked out, her nipples coming erect. His balls tightened painfully in his hand. He squeezed hard, between pain and pleasure. He shifted his grip to his shaft, moving the skin gently up and down.

The tall girl kicked off her sandals. She turned to the mirror and picked up the hem of her short blue skirt, drawing it up to her waist. She wasn't wearing knickers. Richard's breathing became harsh as she put a hand briefly between her legs, covering the black wisp of her hair, and caressed herself.

'Oh shit . . .' Richard almost lost control. He took his hand away and grabbed the arms of the chair, hard. He panted. 'What am I waiting for? Okay . . .'

He staggered to his feet, half bent over with the

hard-on in his pants. Cautiously but quickly, he approached the cubicle curtain. A last look round – no one visible – and he slipped inside.

'Oh, hey, it's Richard.' Little Yuri, dressed but barefoot, put her hands on her hips, swinging her body. 'Richard, is this cool on me?'

Her long, slender legs were bare. A tiny, full, white taffeta skirt barely covered her upper thighs. The dress's waist was nipped in hard with a narrow belt, and the bodice had two shaped white cups and spaghetti-thin straps. Richard's gaze fixed on the two filled cups of her dress: the small, heaving breasts, flushing with a darker amber colour as she watched him look at her.

'That's—' he croaked. 'Cool.'

'Me too?' Keiko's short dress was identical but in buttercup yellow taffeta and lace. Her firm breasts pushed the bodice out further. She had put on fine white pantyhose, and white high-heeled shoes. Modestly, she clasped her hands behind her, her head lowered. Without raising her head, she lifted her dark eyes to Richard. 'Does it look good on me?'

Richard gestured at the hard-on jutting out his pants. He gasped, 'You pass the test!'

Keiko and Yuri giggled together, each putting an arm around the other's waist. Their short taffeta skirts rustled. A warm scent of female bodies filled the cramped cubicle. Heat flushed Richard's body, his arousal growing uncontrollable. He staggered a step forward.

'What about me?' Makiko's voice asked.

Her long black hair was fastened up on the crown of her head now, a few wisps falling down, and she had borrowed another pair of white high-heeled shoes. Apart from those, she was wearing nothing except a short, skin-tight, blue PVC dress. It zipped from the hem up to her cleavage, where a single strap went up around the back of her neck. Two cut-away panels under her arms showed the long, slender curve of her torso, waist and hip. The skin-tight shiny PVC gleamed in the hot cubicle lights as Makiko turned her body from side to side.

'Is it, like, too much?' A disappointed pout appeared.

Richard took her hand and jammed her palm against the front of his trousers. 'Just right!'

All three of them giggled. Yuri put her arm around Makiko's almost-bare waist. Taffeta rustled and PVC creaked. Makiko kept her hand where Richard had put it.

'I guess guys are guys,' she said cheerfully, 'English or not.'

'I guess so . . .' With her free hand, Yuri reached up and began to unbutton Richard's shirt. He reached out and plunged both hands down the front of Keiko's white dress, gripping her small breasts tight in his fists.

She screwed up her face. 'Ow!'

'Oh wow . . .' Leaving his right hand where it was, Richard reached into Yuri's bodice with his left hand, cupping a soft, hot, swelling globe of flesh in the constriction of boned taffeta. The material rustled.

Something that might have been a footstep sounded outside in the shop.

He froze, not daring to move.

'Uh, how much is the red dress?' a stranger's voice drawled. 'Uh-huh. No, I won't try it on, thanks. 'Bye.'

The shop door hissed open, and closed. Richard strained his hearing. A rattle of coat-hangers must mean the assistant was out there somewhere . . .

He freed his hand and put one finger to his lips. Keiko giggled behind her hand. She knelt quickly and began to unzip his fly. His straining erect cock sprang free, into Makiko's waiting hand.

Richard reached out and grabbed Yuri, pulling the girl close. He clamped one hand over her tiny buttocks and thrust the other between her legs. Fiery wetness met his fingers. Under the short taffeta dress, she was naked and knickerless. He began to rub his hand back and forth in her wet cleft, hearing her moan behind clamped-shut teeth. He looked down at Keiko, kneeling in her white dress and pantyhose at his feet, her breasts pushed up out of the bodice of the dress as she leaned forward.

Her tongue darted, licking his scrotum. His balls jerked. Her soft, lipsticked mouth slid over one ball, taking it into her hot wetness, her tongue sliding exquisitely slowly around it.

Makiko's hand closed solidly around his rigid cock. She leaned close, rubbing the head of his hot, swollen member on the PVC dress where it strained taut across her thigh.

'Oh God . . .' Richard groaned. He jammed a finger inside Yuri. The girl moaned ecstatically, her hands reaching for his shoulders. She rubbed the front of her dress up and down his bare chest as she slid her sex up and down on his finger. Her breasts slid out of the dress, her slick skin and hard nipples rubbing against his chest.

On her knees, Keiko's small teeth nipped a tiny fold of his scrotal flesh. His cock throbbed and

131

grew an inch in Makiko's enfolding hand. Tears started from his eyes: he didn't know whether to sob in pain or shoot his load in sheer pleasure. His hand clamped shut on Yuri's tight bum. Makiko bent forward to take the tip of his cock between her red, slick lips.

'That's him, officer! That's the man!'

The cubicle curtains screeched open.

A flood of light illuminated the racks of dresses, the girls, and Richard Stanley with his naked cock out.

'THAT'S HIM!' The same loud female voice screamed. 'He was takin' *drugs* down by the vending machine, I *saw* him!'

The shop assistant screamed.

Richard found himself looking at a big black woman he had never seen before, the clothes-store assistant, and two men in dark uniforms. Police officers.

His erect member deflated instantly to a limp white finger's length.

'I . . .' he said helplessly.

'Will you look at him, he's showin' *dick* to these poor girls!'

Richard turned to appeal to Keiko, Yuri and Makiko.

An elbow caught him hard in the ribs. A bare heel slammed down on his instep, setting him hopping, and he fell into a rail of jackets. It crashed over. Another foot caught him in the stomach as Keiko, Yuri and Makiko giggled, shrieked, and ran.

'Stop them! They're stealing those dresses!' the assistant yelled.

One law officer pelted off after them. Startled, Richard looked down to find the other officer cuff-ing his wrists. 'No, wait – look – this isn't what it looks like! I can explain!'

'They're stealing ma dresses!' the store assistant shrieked.

'But—!' Richard began.

'He's their *accomplice*,' the big black woman stated. Prob'ly he's their *pimp* as well. *I* saw him doin' those pills, I'll say so in the courtroom!'

'But—!' he protested.

The second law officer came in from the mall and shook his head at his partner. There was no sign of Makiko, Keiko, or Yuri.

'I can *explain*,' Richard gasped.

Both men looked at him.

'English,' said one.

The other officer stared down at Richard. 'Are you familiar with the term "Miranda rights"?'

It took forty-eight hours and a call from Edmund Howard to get him on a flight out of LA.

Not before he spent a night in the precinct's holding cells.

Driving him to the airport, Nick Laurie said amiably, 'I didn't think you English guys were so raunchy. Next time you're over here, there's some real hot places I could take you. Some *prime* ass. What do you say?'

'*No!*' Richard Stanley said. 'Never. Ever. *Ever* again. Thank you. I'm not cut out for "raunchy". I'll leave that to – other people. I don't suppose you have such a thing as an aspirin?'

Chapter Nine

THE PHONE WOKE Alix Neville out of a deep sleep.

'What?' Her mouth felt dry. Her hand fumbled the receiver towards her. 'Who?'

'It's me,' Shannon Garrett's voice said over the line.

Alix felt a smile widen her mouth. 'Hi, Shannon,' she said sleepily. 'Hi, boss.'

A glass tumbler fell to the carpet with a thunk. Alix jerked her head up. No mess. It must have been empty. She was lying supine on the sofa. The TV muttered in the corner. The big leather sofa creaked under her as she swung her legs down to the floor.

'Oh, wow . . .' She glanced out of the window. A scattering of brilliant summer stars illuminated the August darkness over the London park beyond her flat. A yellow moon hung low on the horizon. Through the open top of the window, she could smell the green damp of the summer night.

'I guess I fell asleep in front of the TV.' Alix rubbed her neck. Then she stretched her arms, the phone tucked into the crook of cheek and shoulder.

A sense of well-being loosened her muscles.

'Alix, are you there? Are you *awake*?'

'I'm here.' Alix suddenly blinked. 'As for "awake" . . . What time is it?'

'Sorry to call you on a Sunday. Am I too late for you? I'm still in the office.' Shannon's voice became muffled for a second as she spoke to someone off-phone. 'Sorry. Shall I call you back in the morning?'

'God, no. I've got more work on than you'd think possible. Take my mind off it!' Alix's sleepy gaze fell on her desk, where the PC's screen-saver flowed past on the monitor. It was a text saver, using ornate black letters on an olive-green background, and it was scrolling her last encouraging message to herself. Alix watched the unfolding letters flow past – they read: VINCE RUSSELL BEGS LIKE A DREAM.

Alix flopped back on the leather sofa. She wore only a T-shirt and knickers, and the leather was smooth against her bare arms and thighs, and delicately scented. A grin spread irresistibly across her face. 'Yeah . . . he does, too.'

'Alix?'

'I'm here. I'm awake. How's it going with you?'

Shannon's voice over the line became cautious. 'I've pretty much got the October issue to bed. That one might send our sales figures up sufficiently that we'll look good to the accountants.'

Alix found the TV remote by stepping on it, barefoot. She pushed the mute button. An old *film noir* epic flickered silently now in the corner of the room. 'But they won't get those figures until it's too late to make a difference. The bet runs to the end of this month. Hell, we've only got this week left, and I've got a two-day computer conference I have to be at on Tuesday! We'd better get moving. Have you had the next bet down yet?'

There was a momentary silence.

'You could have put it on my e-mail for Monday morning,' Alix added, still looking at her desk. 'Or is it spicy enough to be worth hacking into?'

The silence on the other end of the phone continued.

'Shannon? What is it?'

Shannon Garrett's voice, when it sounded again through the receiver, had a distinctly worried tone. 'Well, I've been notified from upstairs what the next bet is, but I don't know if you'll want to do it. I don't know if it's something you can enjoy.'

Alix scratched through her fine, tangled, silver-blonde hair. She smelled a little of sleep, warm and sweaty, and she stretched again, easing the cramp out of her muscles. 'I guess I will. It seems I enjoy most things! Come on, Shannon – give! What does the bet say?'

'It's quite simple,' Shannon Garrett's voice said. 'It refers to the previous bet. Whichever you were last time – the top or the bottom, the master or the slave – this time you have to take the *other* role.'

Silence.

'It doesn't have to be a return visit to *Pleasure Bound*. It can be anything you like. As long as this time you're the submissive.'

More silence.

'Alix? Hello, Alix? *Hello?*'

A particularly tricky problem with one work-station in the *Femme* office kept Alix occupied until after six on Monday. It also enabled her to avoid speaking to Shannon Garrett.

Tomorrow I'll be out of here – for the next forty-eight hours – and this Friday is the end of the month, and then it's over! No more bets!

And we lose.

The *Femme* office staff began to leave. Alix waved goodnight. The teenage messenger boy, Mike, gave her a quick grin. She stared after his tight bum in its biker's leathers as he strode towards the lifts. *Now that's more like it.*

Alix's full lips curved in a smile as she dusted off her hands and stood up from behind the desk. Maybe I should join him in the lift and just say, 'Boy, I'd sure like to see you naked . . .'

But that isn't the bet, is it?

Alix stretched her arms wearily. Her sleeveless silk vest tautened across her chest, flattening her breasts. She stooped to brush dust from the knees of her ice-blue silk harem pants. As she bent over, a snapshot image appeared in her mind: a figure with its wrists bound, down on its knees – not Vince, this time, but herself . . .

A sudden hot stab of arousal wakened in the pit of her belly.

No . . . I just like the top. Not bottom. Surely?

Footsteps died away into the distance. Summer evening light shone in through the plate-glass windows of the sixth-floor office, illuminating low partitions pinned six layers deep with papers and photo contact-sheets, abandoned swivel-chairs, cute furry toys Blu-tacked to the top of work-station monitors. The whole place smelled faintly of dust, photocopy fluid, and someone's abandoned Nike trainers. On a summer evening like this the building would be emptying, only the

137

security staff compelled to stay on duty—

Alix felt her cheeks heat. She cut the thought off abruptly, all her eroticism chilled and suddenly gone.

No. I am *not* going to go to Vince. Let him find his own submissive!

It's not going to happen, Shannon; get over it!

Alix furiously grabbed her briefcase and her summer jacket and stomped out of *Femme*'s offices, ignoring the lift. Almost too fast for safety, she clattered down the stairs. The floor-length windows on each floor showed her half London – she ignored the view.

What if it wasn't Vince? What if it was just – someone? *How would you feel about being put on your knees* then?

I'd hate it!

Would *you*? *Would you* really?

Alix found herself pushing a wall. It was a blank wall, painted ochre and black, and it didn't have a door in it anywhere. She stopped pushing at the cool plaster and scowled.

This ought to be the way out to the car park!

Alix looked back the way she had come. An identical corridor stretched off into the distance. The stairs back *there*, the lifts over *here* . . . And a number on the nearest door: *201.*

It *is* the way out – two floors below me. Shit, I'm really losing it here!

Alix sighed and turned to retrace her footsteps to the main stairs.

One door stood open. Her head turned automatically as she passed. One of the photo-studios closing up after a shoot. She caught a glimpse of tall white reflector-boards, silver-foil umbrellas,

138

and an expanse of sand-board floor covered with –
with what? Something black, something
leather . . . ?

Alix unconsciously slowed her pace. Several of
the staff photographers knelt down, packing their
gear away into padded cases; and a couple of
women stood around in red silk dressing-gowns,
chatting.

On the stage floor, ropes and cords lay neatly
coiled up beside a thick-handled black bullwhip,
and someone's discarded harness, and a thick
black plastic dildo with a moulded spearhead
glans . . .

'Ms – Neville? Alix?' a pleasant tenor voice
asked.

Alix tore her gaze away from the discarded SM
toys.

A tall, lean, wide-shouldered blond man stood
in the studio doorway. A massive gold signet ring
glinted on his right hand, and the cuff of his shirt
had pulled up enough to show a gold Rolex watch
and the fine gold hairs on his wrist. Unlike the
photographers in their jeans and T-shirts, he wore
a light summer suit.

'Richard Stanley.' Alix didn't offer her hand to
shake. He was several inches taller than her, even
in her heels; she had to look up at him, at his blue-
eyed baby-face under the neat razor-cut yellow
hair. He smelled faintly of cologne. 'I put your
network together last May.' *And you were an asshole
to me.*

'Did you?' Richard Stanley's fair brows lifted.
'No, actually, I recognised you from the videotape
the other day—'

He stopped. Alix's heart thudded. He saw *that*?

And now he wants to gloat—?

'Sorry.' To her amazement, she watched him flush pink from neck to ears. Fair-skinned already, he positively glowed when he blushed. 'Sorry, I didn't mean – Vince told me about you – no, I mean – oh, *shit*.' Richard smiled ruefully. 'I'll just keep digging, shall I?'

'Mmm-huh.' Alix inclined her head, barely able to keep the grin off her face.

Two photographers in blue jeans pushed past, saying good night; the two women – dressed now – followed, one patting Richard on the arm as she went through the door.

'More fun tomorrow!' she said cheerfully.

Alix watched the woman sway off down the corridor, her ripe haunches moving like smooth pistons under her white dress.

'Uh – yeah.' Richard Stanley came to himself. He looked at Alix. 'So, Alix . . . I suppose you're all set to win the next bet for *Femme*?'

Alix's smile faded to ice. She tightened her grip on her briefcase. 'No,' she said grimly, 'you're going to win this one.'

'We are?' He sounded genuinely startled. He stepped back inside the studio, reached for the light-switch, and then hesitated. 'Actually, I have the remains of a bottle of Scotch in the control room; would you like some before you go home?'

Alix hesitated. This is not the Richard Stanley I remember – or at least, it *is*, but without the sheer bloody arrogance that used to get right up my nose. How come? I'd swear this is genuine.

Besides, it'll stop me from thinking about how I'm letting Shannon down.

'Sure.' She hefted her coat and followed Richard

Stanley through the studio into the control room. It was a small anteroom at the back, full of banks of consoles, big enough for two upright chairs and a leather armchair. Richard Stanley waved her to the armchair. He took a bottle from under one of the consoles and rescued two glasses from a shelf.

The door into the studio stayed open. Alix couldn't help looking at the SM gear on the studio floor. A harness with thick black leather straps and silver D-rings seemed designed to buckle around one's hips. In the vee of the leather crotch-piece there was a round hole. Alix realised the equipment was a strap-on dildo.

She sat down in the deep leather armchair and crossed one silk-trousered leg over the other. A little wetness dampened the crotch of her panties.

'Here.'

Alix started. She reached up and took the glass the blond man was offering her. Following the direction of her gaze, he said, 'December's fetish month.'

'I see.' Alix gave the man a hard look. His arrogance seemed to be missing. He was standing, leaning back against the consoles, drink in hand. Long legs in well-cut suit trousers, a narrow waist, and wide shoulders that his suit jacket could not conceal. Her mind, without her will, murmured, *I wonder what he looks like naked*? in her inner ear.

Richard Stanley broke the silence. 'So this bet isn't to your taste?'

She was about to snap something at him. Then, seeing his rueful expression, and puzzled by it, she said quietly, 'No.'

'I know what you mean. Some things are just – too much.' The faint scent of his cologne came to her nostrils. He sat down on the upright chair nearest to her, with his legs apart, elbows on knees, his head down, studying the contents of his glass.

'It isn't the idea of being a slave,' Alix confessed, moved by his open, tired expression. 'It's the idea of Vince Russell crowing over me ... Maybe I wouldn't mind if it wasn't going to be him. I don't want to be *actually* humiliated.'

With no apparent cause, a small flush touched the man's cheeks.

'Are you all right, Richard?'

'Oh – just thinking about something.' He raised his glass and gulped a mouthful of spirit. Alix watched his strong, corded throat. His smooth skin looked soft: would it be silk over iron-hard muscles ... ?

'It's tough for guys too,' Richard Stanley said. He abruptly changed the subject: 'The bet didn't specifically say you had to go to Vince Russell, did it? His didn't mention you.'

'No ... I guess not ...' Alix brightened. 'No.'

She lifted the glass to her lips, and sipped. Single malt stung her mouth. The glass felt warm, taking the warmth of her hand. Someone had switched off the air-conditioning when they left the studio, she guessed. She reached up and hitched her silk vest out of the waistband of her harem pants.

She glanced across the tiny cubicle. The blond man was completely oblivious.

'Before this whole "bets" thing started ...' Richard spoke without looking at her. 'I remember saying to Shannon, *normal people don't do this sort of thing. The average person doesn't dare* ... Of course,' Richard lifted his head and Alix found herself looking into his pale blue eyes, 'of course, I was talking about myself.'

'What happened?' Alix asked.

'Nothing!' He sat bolt upright on the chair. One finger crept up to slide under the collar of his shirt, as if it had become uncomfortably tight.

Alix raised a silver eyebrow at him.

'Oh . . .' Richard Stanley scowled. Something of the malice she remembered from before came back into his expression. 'I flew out to LA before the weekend. I met these three American girls . . .' His scowl deepened. 'We were having sex in a mall—'

'*Where?* How?' Alix wriggled around in the armchair. The leather, hot under her bare arm, stuck to her sweaty skin. 'This sounds good! Tell me about it.'

His ringed hand slammed the glass down on a lighting console, missing sliders by an inch. His face flushed. He glared at her. In the tiny cubicle, his face was no more than eighteen inches from her own. She smelled a sharp tang of male sweat.

'We were in a store,' he said grimly, 'if you must know. A dress store. The changing rooms.'

Alix whooped brattishly. 'Hey! That's what I *call* shopping-and-fucking!'

Richard Stanley made a noise something between a grunt and a snarl. She watched his powerful thighs tense under his suit trousers: he was on the point of standing up and stalking out—

'Actually,' he said, leaning back against the hard-backed chair, and staring over her head, 'we didn't get very far with the "fucking" part. We got discovered. And they ran out on me – you've never seen anything move so damn fast!'

Alix gurgled.

'The little bitches even took the dresses! I had to put them on my credit card before the store owner would drop charges. I came within *this* much of an indecency charge.'

Alix barely got her whisky glass back onto a low shelf, she was shaking so much. 'Oh *shit* . . .'

'*It's not funny!*'

'No.' Alix sat up and bit her lip hard. She dared not look him in the eye. 'Of course not.'

'I wish I had those three little bitches here now!' Richard Stanley snarled. 'I was thinking about that all through today's shoot. All women are bloody bitches!'

Alix wriggled again in the deep chair, her panties creeping up between her legs. Her muscles released tension, her legs going weak. She looked at the seated man's powerful long legs and his broad chest, and she drew in a breath of male sweat and cologne.

She whispered to herself, ' "*It doesn't have to be Vince*" . . .'

'What?' Richard startled, and stared at her.

Alix let her gaze travel through the open door, until she was certain he was looking where she was looking. At the stage floor, and the black leather straps.

'If all women are bitches,' she said, 'then shouldn't you punish one?'

She felt his shocked gaze on her. Her nipples hardened. Since she was not wearing a bra, she felt them push out the smooth silk of her vest: two hard little nubs, perfectly visible.

'That would . . . hardly be in my best interests. For *Babes!*' Richard's mouth sounded completely dry. She turned back to him. His tongue licked at his lips.

A growing bulge packed the front of his pants.

'Sod *Babes!*' Alix said.

A silence.

Richard Stanley's pale blue gaze lifted. He made eye-contact.

'Okay.' He grinned wolfishly. 'Sod *Babes!*. What the hell. Get out there, bitch.'

Now we'll see. Now we'll see if I like this—

Richard Stanley stood, walked out into the studio, and without turning around, snapped his fingers.

Alix struggled up out of the armchair. Her legs buckled. She grabbed at a chair, steadied herself, and walked out into the studio after the man. A hard knot of breathlessness settled under her ribs. Her stomach fluttered. A wet spurt soaked her crotch.

'Ask.' Richard's tone was flint. His blue eyes fixed implacably on her face. 'Beg.'

Alix licked her lips. 'P-punish me . . .'

He stared at her for a long minute.

'You sure?' he asked quietly, in a quite different voice.

Alix's hand dropped to the front of her loose silk pants, rubbing her crotch through the cloth. 'I'm sure.'

'Really?'

Alix surveyed the tall, powerful, well-dressed man – his immaculate suit, expensive jewellery, and spotless tie. A boss, she thought. Definitely a boss. She swayed on her high-heeled sandals.

'In this room, right now – I'm sure.' Alix gave him a brief, open smile. 'Try it outside this room and I'll kick you in the bollocks.'

Richard Stanley nodded, once.

After a pause, he looked her up and down. 'I haven't got those brats here – but I've got you. Down on your knees!'

Alix's stomach pulsed. Slowly, still with her eyes fixed on his face, she sank to her knees. The studio floor was hard. She watched him cross and lock the outside door, then walk slowly and confidently around behind her.

'What—?'

'I didn't say you could talk. In fact . . .'

A big hand grabbed her hair. She felt it twist the long silver mass into a knot at the base of her neck. Alix strained. She couldn't move her head. His other hand came around in front of her, holding something.

'What—' A thick, hard, rubber object was shoved between her lips. Alix found herself unable to move. The gag was stuffed deep into her mouth, pushing back her tongue, and she choked, trying to bend forward, but his hand held her solid and still.

'Www . . .' Alix felt her lips stretched wide around something thick. She tried to purse her lips, feeling textured rubber. Her mouth was stuffed completely full. She felt him belt the strap of the gag at the back of her head. He jerked it tight. The gag forced her jaw even further open.

'If you're wondering,' Richard's voice came from above her, 'that's a cock-gag. Just the thing to keep a woman quiet, a mouth full of cock. Isn't it?'

'Mmpph!' She tried to speak, and succeeded only in straining the strap across her mouth. The moulded rubber cock fixed inside thrust until it was almost down her throat.

Alix lifted her hands to the strap behind her

head. Instantly, her wrists were grabbed, her hands were pressed back against Richard Stanley's full crotch.

'Naughty, naughty. We're not done yet. Get your kit off, you little cow.'

His hands released her wrists. Alix knelt, her hands free, her mouth stuffed full by the moulded gag. She choked but couldn't get a word out.

The man in the executive suit gazed down at her. 'Don't make me tell you twice.'

Alix bit down hard on the rubber cock in her mouth. It hardly gave at all. That she was so utterly silenced made her groin hot. A flush warmed her inner thighs. Slowly she reached down, took the edge of her silk vest and stripped it off over her head. Her naked breasts swelled and flushed as she watched him staring at her.

'You made me give an order twice. You'll be sorry for that.' Richard put his hands on the hips of his tailored jacket. He grinned nastily. 'I can say whatever I want, bitch. I can say I want your hot little cunt. I want to see your hot honeypot, doll. I can tell you I want your little ass bare. And you don't object, do you? Tell me if you object?'

'Mmm!' Alix nodded her head in frustration, her mouth full.

'That's what I thought. Now – *strip*.'

Alix reached for her waistband with shaking fingers. She knelt up, unbuttoning the fastening, and then got to her feet to slide her silk pants down. She bent over to unfasten the ankle-buttons. Her bottom jutted up, protected only by a tiny scrap of red silk.

'There's a tight little ass.' Richard Stanley's big hand suddenly came down on the back of her neck, pinning her bent over. Before she could move, she felt his hand grab the back of her knickers and rip.

She could not move; his hand pinned her with her bare fanny in the air. Warm air, like silk, flowed over her naked wet sex. A finger stroked up between her legs. She became instantly wetter.

'I think you're ready to be punished . . .'

'Gmmmph!'

'But then, you bitches are always ready for it. No. I'm going to make you wait.'

His hand moved so suddenly that Alix stumbled forward. Hands caught her, swinging her up onto her feet. She wriggled her hot ass, her sex aching. If it was only filled like my mouth! she thought, and stared up at Richard Stanley's face. The blond man looked down at her with a grin of anticipation.

'Strip me,' he ordered.

Alix reached up. The palms of her hands were moist and hot. With shaking fingers, she pulled at the knot of his tie. The smooth fabric gave. He was tall enough that without her heeled sandals she had to stand on tiptoe to reach him. Her hot naked body leaned against his shirt-front. She felt the heat of his sweating chest under the thin material.

'Keep going . . .'

Alix dropped her gaze. She unbuttoned his shirt. Slowly she pulled his jacket off his wide shoulders. The creased material of his shirt was damp and warm under her fingertips. She reached down, undid his braces. She began to pull his shirt off, pushing at his lean, muscular arms.

'You're going to do everything I tell you,' his low voice whispered in her ear. 'Without a word of complaint. Shall I tell you how that feels, Alix? I've got a boner you could hang that jacket on!'

She forced herself not to look at his gloating face. Dizzy, breath coming short, she pushed her full naked length up against him, her breasts against his naked smooth chest. His thick pecs pressed against her and she slid her hands down his hot bare belly to the curving hollow of his navel.

'Not so fast, bitch.' His rough hands pushed her back. She couldn't help it, her hot body writhed towards him. He grinned again. 'I said *strip me*.'

Alix took her hands from his stomach's hard, flat muscles. She undid the button of his suit trousers. His groin bulged. She tugged his zip down over his massive erection. His thick cock still hid from her, bulging in his white Calvin Kleins. Frustrated, she stripped his socks and shoes and trousers from his compliant body, and then reached for his pants.

A strong hand grabbed her around the wrist.

'You want it, babe, don't you?'

'Mppprgh!' Alix nodded her head up and down. Her loose silver hair flew about her face, sweat gluing tendrils to her flushed cheeks. Droplets of sweat rolled down her naked body, tracking over the hot skin of her breasts, running down her belly, trickling into her crotch. The rubber cock stuffed her mouth full. 'Mrrhh!'

His other hand grabbed her other wrist. 'Tough shit, babe. Tough shit.'

Alix moaned behind her gag. Her hips writhed with a life of their own. She shifted closer, tried to get her leg up around his hip, to draw his body closer to her. The white underpants were immense

149

with his bulging cock.

He held her out at arm's length. 'Beg.'

'*Mmmpph!*'

'What a shame. Guess you don't want it after all . . .' Richard held her squirming, struggling body effortlessly away from him. 'Then I'll just have to do it myself. But we can't have you interfering.'

Alix shook her head furiously, blinded by her flying hair. She felt her arms forced wide. Something hooked her ankle out from under her. The studio floor thwacked up against her bottom, hard. She gave a muffled yelp. Jolted, breathless, it was a second before she recovered herself, and by then it was too late.

Her left wrist and left ankle were roped together, bending her forward at the waist. They were tied to something – a broom-handle, Alix saw, through sweat-darkened hair. She tugged her right wrist – that was bound, too. Cord tied her right wrist and ankle together.

Richard knelt in front of her. He shoved her right leg and arm unceremoniously outwards. Her thighs spread wide apart. She saw him lash her bound wrist and ankle to the broomstick, and jerked furiously. She couldn't move.

She was tied, helpless, bent forward, hair falling in her face. Her legs and arms stretched out either side. Strain as she could, she could not bring them together. The wooden stake kept her legs stretched wide open, her hot cleft completely exposed.

'Mppgh!' Alix succeeded in rocking herself slightly backwards and forwards. Her hot open sex pressed momentarily against the floor. Her pulse thumped hard in her ears. Her skin flushed, and her chest rose and fell helplessly as she gasped in a breath.

Richard Shannon stood up. He was close enough for her to smell his strong male scent. Her gaze travelled up his long, muscled, lightly furred legs. Sweat sparkled in the fine gold hairs on his calves and thighs. Alix clamped her teeth down on the rubber cock. The smooth line of his thigh vanished under the legs of his white cotton pants. Above the waist his chest swelled out with that triangular male body-line, to the curves of his biceps and triceps.

'Mpph!' Alix's gaze returned to Richard's crotch, a bare eighteen inches away from her. She had to crane her neck up from her bent-over body. Juices poured out of her on to the studio floor, and she moaned again, wriggling her bottom help-lessly. The hard outline of his cock pressed against the white cotton. She saw his bulging scrotum outlined against the fabric beneath. She wrenched at her wrists, wanting to grab his bag with both hands—

'You want it,' Richard said, above her, 'but you can't have it.'

Abruptly his strong hands reached down and jerked down his pants.

His cock sprang free, a stubby thick rod still lengthening even as she watched. His ivory fleshy hardness sprang to attention. Her eyes drank in the smooth, hard, pale arc where it bent slightly forward at the tip, and fixed on the bulging purple head. His glans leaked clear fluid. Alix rolled her spread thighs on the floor, finding no contact, no friction, no release.

'Mppg!' *Bastard!*

The wide, finely haired back of his hand came into view. His strong lean fingers grabbed his own cock, squeezing his hard, hot flesh. Alix's eyes flew open. She thought, I'm going to come without him even touching me—

Richard Stanley turned his back on her.

She made a noise that would have been *fuck!* if it could have got past the thick swell of rubber cock jamming her mouth open. The heat in her sex slid away from climax. Furiously frustrated, she made helpless, outraged, muffled bellowing noises at him, staring up at his tight bum. She thought, I want to shove my finger between his cheeks and right up his ass, I want to *make* him come!

Oh God – agonised – *I* want to come!

The wetness under her smeared the floor. She glared up at him, her bound wrists and ankles throbbing. Water squeezed out of the corners of her eyes and trickled down her cheeks. She clenched her buttocks furiously, trying to force her swollen labia together, but the broom-handle held her spread-legged.

Richard Stanley asked, 'Are you punished?'

'Mppprrgh!'

'Oh, not yet? That's bad, bitch. That's very bad.' His bare feet padded around until he was behind her. She could see nothing but the white reflector-walls and the sand-coloured floor of the studio. Her whole body tensed.

A flash-bulb flared behind her.

'Mmppprg!' she protested. Another flash.

His hard hands pushed through the tangles of her hair, fastening something around her from behind. A wide leather belt, nearly eight inches across. The buckle at the back pulled snug. Bent forward, she could see nothing of what was happening. A sudden tug in the small of her back, the click of a clip snapping home on a D-ring—

Something pulled the wide belt tight around her belly. Alix's bottom left the floor. Her thighs lifted. She tried to wriggle; couldn't. Then her bound heels left the floor, she tipped forward, and she was hanging from a rope suspended over the studio floor, her bound limbs on the wooden pole hanging under her. She lifted her head, looking up through her tangled hair, into the lens of an expensive camera.

Flash.

You shit, you bastard, you utter shit! she yelled. All that came out through the thick rubber cock was a gurgle. Alix found herself twisting slowly as the rope spun. The camera flashed, taking shots of her bare thighs, her dangling naked breasts, and the view of her bare rump, legs held apart, hot fanny exposed.

Wetness poured down her thighs. She wriggled her hips, succeeding only in setting herself revolving again. Her juices trickled down her inner thighs, wetting her sticky skin. Her sex burned with arousal, burning until she longed for something, for anything hard and thick to be jammed inside her.

She heard a click: Richard Stanley fastening the rope's winch.

'If you tell me that's enough punishment,' he said smoothly, 'I'll fuck you. Do you want me to fuck you? Do you want me to take my big thick cock and shove it up you? Do you want me to part those glistening little globes and ram my cock home?'

Alix's head flopped forward.

She hung, held by the centre of the belt at her back, hair trailing down. Tears of frustration poured down her face. Her whole body slumped, only the wooden pole keeping her arms and thighs spread wide. Her skin prickled, tingled. She tried hopelessly to slide a wrist free, wanting to grab her own breasts and squeeze, thrust her fingers up her own fanny.

'That's funny,' he gloated. 'I don't hear you asking.'

Alix lifted her head and gave him a look that would have melted plate glass.

You shit, you fucker, you miserable bastard!

He came and stood in front of her, his naked body entirely exposed to her gaze. A fine sweat glistened on his chest and thighs. His cock lay jutting up flat against his belly, hot flesh in thick gold pubic hair.

He reached behind her head. She swayed gently, suspended, feeling him unbuckle the straps.

He said softly, 'Call me "Master" – just once – and I'll fuck you till you're full.'

The thick rubber gag came out of her mouth.

Alix licked her dry lips, stretching them, wriggling her tongue. She hung, suspended at about the height of his crotch, with her hands and feet tied firmly to the metal pole. She tried to force her thighs together, to rub her wet, red, swollen hot labia together. Her body didn't move an inch. She swung gradually on the rope until she was facing him again.

'Just once,' Richard promised. His naked chest was moving rapidly. One strong hand dropped down to scoop and cup his balls, rolling them in his gold-furred scrotum. 'Beg me once.'

'Master,' Alix said. Her helpless sex pulsed, at his mercy. She felt her clit throb, hardening, a tight, rigid nub of flesh. 'A slave begs – fuck me! Fuck me! Fuck me, Master, fuck me now!'

Her spread thighs loosened, tightened. Her bound arms and legs tensed. Her sex dripped hot juice, she heard it spatter on the floor. Her flesh swelled and hardened unbearably. In front of her, an inch or two away, his thick sex-scented cock hardened and swelled another inch. Without the least preparation her body was swung around on the rope. Dizzy, spinning, light-headed, she felt his hard hands grip her hot naked hips, his fingers digging hard into her skin—

'Have this, bitch!'

Without even a moment's warning to brace herself, Alix felt her body rammed back against his. The tip of his cock jammed her labia apart. She threw her head back and yelled ecstatically. His shaft slipped up her, his girth forcing her apart, her hot flesh swelling and clamping around him. His strong hands shoved her away, forward, then his fingers fixed under the edge of the belt around her waist and slammed her back again.

'Oh yeah! *Fuck* me!'

With her bound arms stretched, her dangling breasts bouncing, Alix felt herself shoved out and back, forward and back, each time the weight and thick solidness of his cock thunking right up inside her. His hot, hard belly slapped her buttocks. His balls banged against her pussy. The friction in her sex grew unbearable, pouring wet—

'I'm coming!' Richard yelled behind her. 'Oh God, oh *God*—!'

155

His agonised yell of pleasure shattered any control she had left. His thick spurting cock jammed solidly up her, up to the hilt, thrusting, banging, squelching his hot come over her fanny and spread thighs.

Alix screamed. Pleasure flooded her body, searing pleasure jolted out from her clitoris, her sex convulsed, and she came doubly, came hard, came strong; came so hard that she spurted her juices back over him, soaking his cock and wet hair and hard belly; came until she threw back her head, the only part of her body she could move, her wet hair flying, as she shrieked in compelled release.

A little while later, dressed and about to leave, Alix saw Richard Stanley, also dressed, fiddling at the back of one of the camera tripods.

'Don't,' she protested.

The fair-haired man looked up at her. 'I was going to destroy the negatives. I thought . . .'

'Oh, yes. Of course.'

Alix gave him a wicked grin as she reached the studio door.

'But *not* before you've made me a full set of prints.'

Chapter Ten

RICHARD SAT STILL for a long time after the studio door closed behind her.

His body glowed in relaxed warmth as he sank back in the black leather-upholstered chair. It creaked faintly. The control room's shelved walls, covered with lighting consoles and banks of photographic equipment, made the place seem small and secure.

That was – was – that was ... amazing.

Richard shook his head disbelievingly. He ran his hand through his short hair. Cooling sweat made his scalp sticky. He scratched his armpits, stretched his arms, and yawned immensely. The residue of warmth in his groin glowed.

He sat up, rummaging behind a filing cabinet, and rescued the bottle of single malt. Then he sat and sipped. The whisky slid, burning, over his tongue and down his throat.

That woman is quite something.

Slowly he began to button his shirt, one button at a time. His tie was still in the studio, he realised. But it was late, no one would see him leaving the Midnight Rose International building without his tie ...

His fingers stopped on the top shirt-button. He frowned.

Why the fuck, Richard thought in bewilderment, *did I just help her win the bet?*

Because she offered. And because you wanted to!

Richard Stanley slammed the whisky glass down on the filing cabinet, ignoring the splash of liquid over a stack of grainy black-and-white photographs.

What a story to tell the guys – and I can't! What am I supposed to say? This woman wanted me to have wild, wild sex with her, so I did, and I'm sorry it lost you your *jobs*, guys, but hey, that's the way the cookie crumbles . . . Oh, *shit*. The windowless, cluttered room was suddenly less of a refuge.

And they *are* going to hear about it. She's going to report back to Edmund Howard. Nothing's ever safe from gossip in this place! I'm going to go down in company history as the man who got *Babes!* deep-sixed with his cock . . .

Richard felt his scrotum tightening. A *frisson* brought the shaft of his penis half-erect in his trousers. A fugitive thought slipped from his mind as fast as he realised it was there – he drained the glass of the remaining whisky and sat with his head in his hands: *that was an idea, what was it?*

Slowly it came back to him. *What if you used your cock to save yourself?*

Almost against his will, his rod stiffened. He wiped his hand over his face. A thin film of sweat covered his skin. The tips of his fingers felt cold. A thump of adrenaline chilled the pit of his belly.

Alix found someone to be her master, and she enjoyed the hell out of it. So she wins.

I can't guarantee that Vince Russell will find anyone tonight to be his slave – so he'll never know if he gets off on being the top, so he'll lose the bet.

But not if I go and tell him I'll bottom for him.

Not if I go down there to the security office, right now, and – offer.

Now his hands went cold. Richard gazed down at his fingers. They shook. Not with fear, but with the anticipation of an unadmitted – inadmissible – desire. *I'm not* really *going to do this, am I?*

I gave Vince Russell a right bollocking. I'm sure there's nothing he'd like better than to have the situation reversed.

Richard's mouth went dry. A sudden picture of the bullet-headed man flashed into his mind: burly, strong, ex-army; now down there in his security uniform, all alone in the office. Richard looked down into his lap.

A rigid erection poked up the cloth of his suit trousers.

That can't be because – not twice in one evening – I can't want to – not *that*!

Oh hell . . .

Richard Stanley reached across to the telephone and stabbed at the buttons. 'Security? Good. No, no problems. Who's on night duty tonight? I see. And Vince Russell? Ah. I see . . . Has he left the building yet, do you know? *Right*. Thank you.'

Richard put down the phone, staggered upright and hobbled as swiftly as he could out of the studio, down towards the underground car park.

There were only a few cars still remaining in the car park now. Dusk was falling. Harsh strip lighting glowed white, reflecting in the wide stretches of rainwater on the concrete floor and the oil-stains from previously parked vehicles. Richard stood still, listening. No engines. A distant roar from the road out of Canary Wharf; a boat hooting on the river. A gull shrieked.

Close at hand, a car door opened.

Richard Stanley walked briskly around the edge of the lift building. The low roof seemed to press down on him, his breath was tight in his throat. A cold knot settled in his solar plexus. The single car on this side of the park was a rusted Astra estate. Bent over the open boot, Vince Russell was pulling out a sports bag. Obviously it must contain his casual clothes as he was still in his work uniform.

Richard became conscious of his clean, pale grey Armani summer suit, his crisp shirt and expensive shoes, and the smell of his own cologne. The magazine-picture of a sharp young executive . . . Chill wind, blowing between the car-park floors, ruffled his short fair hair as he strode on.

'Vince!'

The big man straightened up out of the estate's boot. A blank expression appeared on his strong features. 'Sir?'

Richard opened his mouth to speak. No words came.

Vince Russell put down the sports bag he was holding. His heavy work boots were scuffed, Richard noted. The uniform cap and PTT radio rested on the Astra's roof; but the security guard's handcuffs were still fastened to his heavy-duty belt. His shirt-collar button was undone, showing a clump of dark chest-hair. Richard let himself notice how Vince Russell's biceps strained the

160

sleeves of his uniform jacket.

'Yes, sir?' the big man prompted.

Richard put his hands behind his back, attempting to look imperturbable. 'About your participation in the latest bet – any success?'

His heart in his mouth, Richard momentarily hoped to hear the other man say 'yes', and give details. Vince Russell lowered his head. Shadows from the car-park lighting made his expression grim.

'Nothing so far, sir,' he said.

'You've only got until tomorrow morning!' It came out sounding like a reproach; he was not surprised to see Russell flush, and stare aggressively.

'I thought I might go up west tonight.' Russell shrugged powerful shoulders. 'Sir.'

A wealth of cynicism sounded in that 'sir'. Richard suddenly felt his white-collar job and his class very keenly. He blurted, 'You needn't do that.'

Vince Russell scowled, obviously puzzled. 'Don't get it, sir.'

'You needn't go up to the West End.' Richard sought Vince's gaze, meeting the dark-brown eyes of the other man. He swallowed. Dizzy, he said, 'You could stay here. Right here.'

The ex-soldier's expression remained puzzled. As Richard watched, the man's face cleared. He looked Richard up and down, from neatly cut hair to polished shoes. Richard felt his face getting hot. Worse, he felt his cock stir in his pants.

'You're joking' Vince Russell said bluntly. 'You're fucking joking, aren't you. It's a wind-up.'

Beyond the concrete walls, the sky gave up the last of its sunset glow. The wind blew colder between the car park's open floors. Somewhere a distant door slammed, bringing Richard's heart into his mouth.

He held Vince's gaze, shook his head. 'I'm not joking. *You need to know if you get off on being a top.* A master. That's the bet. And I'm – here.'

'No shit?'

Vince Russell moved very fast, very quiet; he was in Richard's face before Richard knew it, the big heavy male body looming up at him. Richard opened his mouth to speak, and Vince Russell's hand clamped over his crotch.

'No shit . . .' the uniformed man drawled. He looked into Richard's eyes. Richard remained perfectly still. His cock, trapped in the thick blunt male fingers, twitched. Vince Russell slowly nodded. 'So. Mr Stanley. Here you are . . .'

Abruptly, Vince Russell let go. He spun on his heel and walked back to the Astra estate. Without looking round, he growled, 'I'll take my chances up west, thanks.'

'It won't go on your record.' Richard stumbled over getting the words out.

Something in his tone must have struck the other man as painfully honest. Vince Russell stopped and turned round. He looked across the concrete at Richard Stanley. His dark brows lifted, questioningly. Richard pressed his lips together, and gave a firm nod.

'You sure?' Vince Russell did not mean whether it would go on record, Richard saw. There was a visible pressure behind the fly of the security-uniform trousers. His own legs began to shake, muscles jumping.

Richard Stanley drew himself up and managed

to give Vince a completely supercilious stare. He said sharply, and with immense superiority, 'Okay, you're not up to it. I thought as much. I should never have picked you for this – it needs someone with balls. Not some pencil-dick yob.'

Vince Russell grinned nastily. 'Yob, is it?'

'And don't be insolent,' Richard snapped. Or you'll be in my office first thing tomorrow morning.'

He swung around and began to walk briskly towards the lift doors. Two steps, three – he heard nothing, but suddenly his legs went out from underneath him. He had just time to realise he had been kicked as he plunged forward. His hands skidded out from under him and he sprawled full-length in a pool of old black oil on the concrete.

A knee jammed solidly in the small of his back. His jacket flew open, oil soaking into his shirt. He felt his right wrist grabbed and wrenched behind his back. A thunk, and solid metal whipped painfully over his wrist-bone: the cuff snapped shut. The sound was loud above his gasps.

Richard writhed his body, trying to wrench himself out from under Vince Russell's pinioning knee. He felt a slackening in pressure from above. If he used his full strength, he would be free.

He let his body go limp. His other wrist was swiftly seized, and cuffed in the small of his back. The cold sticky oil oozed out from under his prone body, marking his grey suit and white shirt irretrievably. Cold, hard wet concrete pressed against his throbbing crotch.

A powerful hand seized his shoulder and rolled him onto his back.

Vince Russell stared down at his supine body.

163

He reached out with a boot and prodded Richard's ruined suit. 'Not so smart now, are we, sir?'

'You can't do this to me!' Richard felt the cold of the concrete bite into his shoulders and buttocks. The crotch of his trousers was smeared thick with oil, clammily sticky against his swelling cock. His skin shivered with violent arousal. His mouth went dry as he protested, 'Damn you, Russell, what do you think you're doing?'

'I'm fucking you, *sir*.' The uniformed man put his big fists on his hips, looking down at the sprawled form at his feet. 'In fact, I've had just about enough of your lip – I'm going to give you a damn good hiding, Mr Stanley, and there isn't a damn thing you can do about it.'

'No!' Richard whimpered, shocked. 'Not that. You can't do *that*.'

'Can't I? I can do anything I like.' Vince Russell's head lifted; he gazed around the dark, deserted car park. 'You can scream your head off. It won't help you. There's a lot of things I can do to you while you're in cuffs.'

He returned his gaze to Richard and smiled a particularly nasty smile. 'Bit of a shame if you change your mind halfway. You're not going anywhere.' His tone dropped to a growl. 'You've been the high-and-mighty boss for far too long – now I'm going to teach you a lesson you'll never forget.'

Richard dug his heels into the concrete, trying to push his body away from the man who towered over him. The concrete rasped his shoulders. A seam ripped in his suit. One of his shoes dragged off. Vince Russell stepped forward and kicked his legs apart.

'I'm *your* boss now,' he stated. 'And you're going to do everything I tell you to. I frighten the piss out of you – *don't I?*'

'Yes,' Richard whispered.

'Yes what?'

'Yes, *sir*.' He stared up from where he lay, oil-smeared and spread-legged. He tried to wrench his arms free of the cuffs. The metal bit into his flesh. His own body-weight pinned him down. He was helpless to move. 'I'll make you pay for this!' Richard turned his head away. The dark car park stretched away on all sides. Humiliation burned in him.

He felt his cock slowly but surely begin to harden.

'I think you're protesting too much.' Vince Russell dropped swiftly to one knee, and groped Richard's crotch. 'Yeah. I thought so. You lied to me.'

'I'm sorry,' Richard whispered, not looking at him. 'Sir.'

'That's more like it.'

Powerful hands grabbed the front of Richard's belt. He was dragged up onto his feet so fast it left him breathless. He stared into Vince Russell's face, mere inches away. In the long pause, Richard saw in the Astra's window the reflection of Richard Stanley, suit smeared thick with black sump oil, hair sticking out, face bright red, one shoe missing, hands cuffed behind him. Slowly but surely, his cock crept upwards, the shaft thickening and growing.

Vince Russell's fist knotted in the top of Richard's trousers pulling him up onto his toes, wet fabric jerked up sharply between his legs.

165

'Who's a naughty boy, then?' he grinned.

'Me, sir. Sorry, sir.' Richard found there was no need to think about playing his role. The improvisation came naturally. As he realised that, his cheeks reddened still more. Very quietly, he said, 'I gave you a stiff reprimand, Vince. Are you going to punish me?'

'You didn't say "sir".' Vince Russell's hand dropped to his heavy-duty leather belt. He jerked the buckle open and pulled it free of his belt-loops.

'Sorry, sir!' Richard licked his lips, swaying on his feet. The look in Vince Russell's brown eyes was thoughtful. Nothing is keeping me here, Richard thought suddenly. I could run. More than that – if I asked him to unlock these cuffs, he would.

Or *would* he?

The possibility that Vince Russell might not want to let him go – that he might actually be as helpless, as trapped as he seemed – made Richard's hot throbbing cock jut painfully up.

'Punish me,' he whispered. 'I deserve it, don't I?'

Vince Russell doubled the leather strap, holding the buckle, and slapped the loop into the palm of his other hand. Richard's cock jumped. The big man let go of the fabric, reached out, and unzipped Richard's fly. He jerked trousers and underpants down together to Richard's knees. Then he jerked his thumb at the Astra.

'Over the bonnet.'

'What?' Richard exclaimed. He stood naked from the waist down, the wind chilling his unprotected crotch.

'Bend over!' Vince snarled, grinning nastily. 'Every time I drive this baby in the future, I'm going to be remembering you bending over it.

166

Now move!'

Richard stood quite still for a second. Then he hobbled over to the Astra, and – his hands still cuffed behind his back – leaned forward until he fell, sprawling across the cold metalwork.

Whack!

The blow caught him unprepared. The thick leather belt bit deep into his bum. Pain flared across his bare buttocks. He writhed, his head coming up and back with astonishment. His cock, crushed flat against the shiny paintwork, throbbed and swelled and jutted instantly erect.

Whack!

'Oh God!' he sobbed. His body glowed. His buttocks were numb. Blood thundered through his veins. Blood engorged his penis until his erection was agonising. 'Punish me! Vince! Master! Please!'

Whack!

His wet, oil-smeared body slid on the car's unyielding bonnet; he humped his hips up to meet the blow; the leather smacked his ass, and he came across the freezing metalwork. 'Oh *yes!*'

Richard slumped, sweating and shuddering, his body so hot that he could no longer feel the cold wind. His cheek pressed against the hard cold metal. Sweat ran down his face, his hair plastered to his forehead. Aftershocks of pleasure shuddered through his body.

Silence.

Dirty, wet and humiliated, Richard Stanley lay on the concrete of the car park.

Vince Russell, down on one knee beside him, stretched out a hand and put it on his oil-stained shoulder. Quietly, he said, 'You want to call it a day, mate?'

Richard bit his lip. He was about two foot from one of the most impressive hard-ons he'd ever seen: Vince Russell was *big*. He looked at the throbbing juicy cock.

'I think you've won,' Richard said huskily. He smiled, eyes wet. 'I think you get off on being a master – sir.'

'Yeah.' Vince was momentarily thoughtful. 'I guess I do.' A pause. He chuckled gruffly.

A tiny click.

The cuffs slid off.

Richard Stanley sprawled face down in the oil and water, in his ruined clothes. When Vince rolled him over, he had a beatific smile on his face.

'That ought to get you home.' Vince looked critically at his spare track suit, hanging baggily on Richard Stanley.

'Thanks.' Richard moved stiffly, his ass sore.

Vince Russell remained standing beside his car. When Richard looked curiously at him, he shuffled his feet and stared off into the middle distance.

'I just wondered,' Vince said.

'What?'

'Well. I just. You don't seem—' The big man finished zipping up his chinos. He wouldn't look at Richard. In a burst, he said, 'It doesn't bother you that you got off on being a bottom?'

Richard shrugged. 'It doesn't bother you that you got off on being a top.'

'No, but . . . but I'm a man. I'm *supposed* to! Not the other way!'

Richard retrieved his car keys from his ruined

suit. 'You certainly seemed to like the reverse of this, if that *Pleasure Bound* tape's anything to go by.'

'Maybe it depends who's doing it—' Vince Russell cut himself off abruptly.

Richard didn't hear; his mind was on the earlier part of the day.

'Well – so far, I make that another draw. Four days to go.'

Chapter Eleven

SHANNON GARRETT WALKED briskly and completely absent-mindedly through the London streets. The most recent report on a completed 'bet' had come down late from the top floor. It had her thunderstruck. Vince Russell and *Richard Stanley*. . .

He did that? He *really* did that? *Richard* did that?

The day was hot, sweaty, sticky. Heat lightning flash-bulbed over distant rooftops. Hard paving-stones jarred under her high-heeled shoes, and her crisp white cotton blouse clung to her damp waist. Shannon's mind whirred.

Maybe he's got some hidden agenda – but if he has, I can't see what it could be. But there has to be something in it for him! I know that man. He doesn't *do* generous . . .

Her feet carried her through, and then out of, the square mile of the City. Her attention didn't register traffic.

Several black cabs blasted their horns.

'And you!' Shannon retorted, coming to. She realised she was wandering diagonally across the road in Great Russell Street. 'Ah – right. Sorry . . .'

A lurid yellow haze of cloud hung in the sky. Sauna-sunlight shone on the whitewashed fronts of the exclusive shops and on the dusty leaves of the plane trees. Flakes of bark covered the pavement, along with pigeon droppings and sweet wrappers. There was a faint sleepy smell of petrol and sweat. People in their dozens pushed past her.

Shannon stepped smartly up onto the pavement. She glanced at her wristwatch. Two o'clock. 'Shit,' she muttered. A burly West German tourist and his wife gave her a sharp look as they passed. She moved closer to the wall on the opposite side of the pavement. Black-painted railings jutted above her head. Bright posters advertising exhibitions hung on them – she was, she realised, standing outside the British Museum.

Her cotton blouse's short sleeves were wet and dark with sweat under the arms of her light suit jacket. Electric air shifted in the London street, and the fine hairs on her forearms prickled. Now that she had stopped walking, she realised that the muscles of her legs ached. Her mouth felt thick and dry with thirst.

Julia can cope without me for another hour, she thought. I'm already late back. A cold drink won't make much difference one way or the other. Don't they have a café in the museum? I'm sure I remember one . . .

Shannon walked up to the gates and into the courtyard in front of the museum. A cluster of Japanese tourists were taking photos of the neo-classical frontage. The white steps were spotted with the muted pastels of girls in summer dresses and the milk-blue faded jeans of male students on

171

holiday. Everyone in casual dress, it seemed; not her own office-wear . . . She straightened her back and walked wearily up towards the main entrance, opening her tiny clutch-bag to the security guard's stare. The cool and welcome shade of the portico fell across her.

A black cab, passing the British Museum gates, screeched to an abrupt halt.

'I'll walk from here,' Richard Stanley said hastily.

The cab driver gave him the look reserved for customers who ask for an address in Canary Wharf and then claim to be walking there from Great Russell Street. Richard shoved a tenner at him and scrambled out of the cab, completely forgetting to ask for a receipt for expenses. The taxi screeched off.

He shaded his eyes against the darkening yellow light.

There. The unmistakable, uncontrollable mass of brown-red curls, bobbing away through the crowds at the top of the steps and into the museum itself. A glimpse of an ivory-white skirt and the long, slender, pale line of her calf. Shannon Garrett, no doubt about it.

Without asking himself why he was doing it, Richard began to walk smartly after her. Two security guards at the museum gates were drowned in a mass of tourists asking questions. He strode across the courtyard.

The sky was completely clouded over now. Sultry heat made him sweat under his summer jacket. As he put his foot on the first of the steps, a coin-sized dark splatter kicked up dust – a raindrop. Then two more droplets; five; a dozen . . . a summer shower broke from the London sky.

Richard moved swiftly up to the entrance, elbowing his way between tourist couples. Brown curls reflected in one set of glass doors. Shannon! He pushed through the crowd as the summer rain began in earnest and caught a glimpse of her turning down the left-hand ground-floor corridor.

Okay, I won't lose her now . . .

More confident now that he was in the same building with her – it was unlikely she could walk back past him without him noticing – he strolled down the corridor, past the museum bookshop. His eyes searched the crowd. No one wearing a raw-silk tailored ivory skirt and jacket. No one among the visitors had tumbling chestnut-red curls. No Shannon Garrett.

At the point where a private gallery branched off, with a notice advertising an exhibition of angels, Richard stopped. Supposing she had gone in there? Or supposing he did, and she hadn't, and he missed her?

What am I *doing*?

He wiped the heel of his hand across his forehead. A fine sweat slicked his skin. He could feel his face heat. Following her, following his rival editor, actually stopping a cab when he caught a glimpse of her—

'I'm losing it,' he muttered.

Tension left his body in a rush. Richard wiped his face again with the silk handkerchief from his jacket pocket, and then took his jacket off and slung it over his shoulder. The museum's air-conditioning cooled the air pleasantly. Quiet voices echoed between the mosaic-covered walls, the visitors here numerous but less hectic than outside.

What was I going to *say* to her? God knows. This whole idea was stupid in the extreme. Thank God I didn't catch up with her.

He was turning to leave when he thought, *I'm thirsty. Didn't that sign say there was a café down here somewhere?*

A few yards further on he came to the blond-wood frontage of the museum's café. He went in. A buzz of voices overrode the background music. The entrance walkway was slightly raised, and he found himself looking down at several tables under the clerestory windows.

One woman sat alone, directly beneath him. The neck of her white blouse was unbuttoned under her jacket. Red-brown curls covered her slim shoulders. From where he stood, both hands gripping the wooden rail, Richard Stanley looked straight down her cleavage, at the round globes of her breasts encased in the lacy white cups of her bra. Tiny droplets of sweat dappled the swelling curves. He wondered what it would taste like to lick her skin, plunge his tongue deep into her cleavage . . . take the cool glass of wine on her table and tip it down the front of her blouse and then lick her dry—

The woman raised her head, looking up and back.

'*Richard!*' Shannon Garrett exclaimed. 'What are you doing here?'

Shannon shifted her café chair so that she could look up at Richard Stanley without straining her neck. The blond man had one blunt-fingered hand resting on the wooden rail. His nails were square-cut and clean. The jacket of his steel-grey silk

174

Armani suit was slung casually over one shoulder, and it drew her eye. He was lean-hipped, lean-bodied, but now she looked, his shoulders under the crisp white shirt were very broad.

He reached up and took his jacket off his shoulder, folding it over one arm and holding it in front of him. 'Uh, Shannon . . . I . . .'

Shannon suddenly noticed the direction of his pale blue gaze. From where he stood above her, he was undoubtedly getting a very good view down her shirt. She pressed her lips together, biting back a comment.

But then – I'm not ashamed of how I look!

Shannon swivelled round, away from the café table, and crossed her legs. Her lined raw-silk skirt slid back from her knee, exposing several inches of smooth thigh in nude stockings.

An elderly couple entering the café pushed past Richard. He put one hand out to grab the wooden rail. It was the arm over which he had slung his jacket. As the jacket moved, Shannon found herself face to face with Richard's crotch through the bars of the railing.

He dressed to the left, obviously. The bulge of a semi-hard-on pushed out that side of his trousers, prominent against his inner thigh. As he saw her notice it, his cock jumped and swelled against his fly.

Hastily he held his suit jacket back in front of him.

Shannon continued to look up at him, with a slight smile.

'Yes?' she said sweetly.

Richard Stanley, with a sudden cocky grin, murmured down at her, 'I suppose you've been hearing things about me from Alix.'

'Oh, yes. And I've been hearing things about you and *Vince* . . .' Shannon let the sentence trail off.

It worked better than she could have imagined. Red heat crept up to his ears, down his neck. His face positively glowed.

'Ah. Yes.' Richard Stanley cleared his throat. He looked away from her for a moment, gazing at the crowded café. Music played, the whitewashed walls gleamed, and the light from outside was turning bruise-coloured: a summer storm pattering on the windows.

On impulse, Shannon pushed a second chair out from the café table, invitingly.

Richard descended the walkway steps and joined her at the table, seating himself with care. Shannon noted that he kept his jacket across his lap. She imagined his thick cock pressing against the crotch of his trousers, entangled in his underpants . . .

She reached up and slid her thumb down the vee of her open blouse. Just short of indecent, the fine cotton stretched smoothly across her bare upper breasts. Her blouse opened far enough to show the warm lift and fall of her breasts as she breathed quickly. She felt her nipples swell in her bra cups, jutting hard nubs rubbing against the soft cotton arousing her further.

I wanted to drive *him* crazy, Shannon thought. Not myself!

Not that he's bad-looking. It's just a shame he's such an asshole.

'Why did you do it?' she asked suddenly. 'Vince reported you came and – offered. Why?'

She was surprised to see humour in his blue-grey gaze.

'You know me.' Richard Stanley shrugged insouciantly. 'Anything for Mr Howard. Anything for the magazine.'

'Okay – but helping *Alix* didn't help *Babes!*, did it? Offering to do that was only useful to *Femme*. You know that.' Shannon shook her head in frustration. 'So why did you do it?'

'You have to *ask*? You've seen that girl! And after I'd done that, well . . .' Another lift of those powerful shoulders under his cream-coloured, expensive, and extremely well-cut shirt. He scrubbed his free hand through his short, neat blond hair, obviously embarrassed. 'Going to Vince, that just seemed . . . I don't know . . . *fair*, I suppose.'

It was the last thing she expected him to say. She studied his serious face. He was undoubtedly being genuine, caught in what he plainly felt to be embarrassing honesty. Shannon thought, good grief! That *is* why he did it. Because it was fair to even up the score.

Shannon, amazed, gave Richard Stanley a very hard stare. 'You're a strange man, Richard.'

'So I've been told.' A glint of cocky humour showed in his eyes.

Shannon leaned forward, putting her elbows on the table. Her heavy breasts shifted, her cleavage deepening. Warmth brought out the musk of her perfume. She said quietly, 'Did you enjoy it?'

'Did I what?'

Shannon said each word clearly and distinctly, although quietly enough that the people at the next table could not overhear: 'Did you enjoy being a slave to a man?'

177

She watched as Richard Stanley squirmed in his chair.

'No. Yes. I think – no.' Richard put his jacket across his lap and rested both his hands on the blond-wood table-top. Then he looked her straight in the eye. 'But it made me come.'

A pulse of arousal went through Shannon's groin. She felt the lips of her labia harden and swell. The smooth wood of the chair-seat was hard under her crotch. She parted her thighs fractionally, pushing herself down. Her panties pressed up against her, sticky and wet.

'I wouldn't do it again,' Richard said, 'but I'm glad I did it once. So I guess I win the bet as well as Vince.'

'Alix and Vince,' Shannon mused. 'Those two get all the luck, don't they?'

'Not necessarily . . .' He smiled. He had clear, boyish skin and even white teeth. Out of the office, on his own, he had a good smile: unguarded, and with a hint of self-deprecation.

Richard Stanley lifted one hand off the café table-top. He reached out and hooked one broad finger down the front of her blouse, and tugged forward.

Shannon glanced frantically around. No one in the café was looking. Her blouse and jacket strained forward. His finger was down between her breasts, hooked over the front fastening of her bra. His insistent pull both forced her breasts together, compressing them, and gave him an uninterrupted view down her front.

'What do you think you're doing!' she hissed.

'I'd like to eat my dinner off you,' he said, a thick catch in his voice. His blue gaze held hers. 'And you wouldn't have to chain me down for me to do whatever *you* wanted, either.'

Shannon, leaning forward, slid her hand under the table, on to Richard's leg, and up under his jacket. She felt a hot bulge. Carefully, she closed her fingers around the thick girth of his cock, feeling it leap under the expensively tailored cloth.

'Let's—' *Go somewhere*, she was about to say. A klaxon suddenly drowned out her voice.

'THIS IS AN URGENT ANNOUNCEMENT. WILL ALL VISITORS PLEASE LEAVE THE MUSEUM! THIS IS A SECURITY ALERT! PLEASE WALK *SLOWLY* TO THE NEAREST EXIT. THERE IS NO NEED TO PANIC. PLEASE LEAVE THE MUSEUM IMMEDIATELY!'

Shannon snatched her hand away from his lap. Equally suddenly, Richard took his finger out of her cleavage. A rising buzz of voices turned to shouts, tourists yelling, white-coated kitchen staff streaming towards the exit—

Tell them there's no need to panic! Shannon thought dizzily, still in the throes of arousal. And I guarantee they'll run! What on earth . . . It's just another false alarm, I'd bet money on it, but what a moment for it to happen!

A woman in a red dress shoved past, knocking the table against Shannon. Shannon gasped, air squeezed out of her body. Before she could do more than think *I'm trapped*!, Richard Stanley swung the table bodily away from her and pulled her up onto her feet by one hand.

'It won't be anything! It never is,' Shannon snarled, frustrated.

'No. It never is.' His blue eyes lit up. 'Here.'
'What?'

One of his broad hands went over her mouth. His other arm went round her waist, lifting her feet off the floor. She grabbed at him, arms flailing. He took two steps back to the wall, out of the crowd, swept her legs out from under her, and dropped.

The impact knocked the breath out of her.

Feet clattered past.

She was lying on the floor beside Richard, clamped close to his body, hidden under the long bench table in the café's corner. The floor tiles shocked her flushed skin with their ceramic coldness. His arms were around her from the back, pressing her back to his chest, her rump to his crotch. She wriggled. His thick cock poked insistently at his trousers, jutting into the cleft between her silk-clad buttocks.

Silence.

'They've gone—'

'Wait!' he hissed.

Shannon heard the café doors open. She froze. What if they were discovered? Security men's voices yelled, not six feet away from her. What could she *say* if found hiding under a table with a man? A man with his bulging cock erect in his pants?

A delicious warmth heated her inner thighs, her hips and her belly. Her labia stiffened again. A uniformed leg and boot paused beside the table. From his stance, it was clear the man was looking out into the room.

Richard's hand slid down the front of her shirt, stroking her stomach under the sweat-soaked cotton blouse. His fingers pushed further under the waistband of her skirt, between the buttons of her shirt, and contacted bare belly-skin. She bit her lip. A faint mew escaped her. She froze again.

The uniformed legs turned this way and that. Shannon bit at her lip.

Richard's finger slid under her plain garter-belt and under the front of her panties. The pad of his finger found her clit, circling so softly, so teasingly softly . . . her hips jerked.

'Kitchen's clear!' a distant voice yelled. 'You clear in there, Frank?'

The blunt fingertip pushed into her damp pubic hair. It pushed down, and in, until it shoved in between the folds of her hot, soaking-wet flesh. Shannon clamped both her own hands over her mouth. She tried to push her hips forward and up so that he could reach further into her sex. The thick tip of his cock poked into her back, through the fabric of his trousers.

'All clear!'

The voice bellowed directly above her. Shannon started. Richard's finger stuffed itself up inside her. Her muscles spasmed in a tiny, exquisite orgasm. She flopped breathlessly and silently back against the blond man's body.

The sound of the café doors slamming echoed through the building.

Shannon heard a key turn in the lock outside.

She lay still, breathing quietly, for several more seconds. Then she rolled out of Richard's embrace and got to her feet.

The white-walled café was completely empty. A blue-purple sky full of storm-clouds shone beyond the clerestory windows. Rain drummed on the glass, running down in diamond ripples. No one had turned off the music. A faint thread of Delius murmured in the background.

The cash-tills stood empty. Through the open kitchen doors, Shannon saw that the kitchens were deserted. Display food stood on show, untouched now that the customers were gone. She turned slowly, full circle, her skin tingling from head to foot with the thought, *We are alone. We can do whatever we want*.

'No one saw us hide.' Richard Stanley's voice came from behind her. He was standing up, she saw when she turned, and brushing the dust from his crumpled suit trousers. His jacket lay abandoned on the tiled floor. He met her gaze deliberately. 'No one knows we're here, Shannon.'

Shannon turned on her high heels, walking between the display cabinets: shelves of food, appetisers, main courses, and desserts. Without looking back, she said, 'I thought you wanted lunch.'

His voice said, 'I'm hungry if you are.'

'I'm hungry.' Shannon stopped by the display of desserts. Rows of custards, chocolate mousses and gâteaux confronted her. She turned around, swinging her hips. She rested the edge of her bum against the tray-shelf and put her hands behind her, leaning slightly back on them. She crossed one ankle over the other. The position thrust her upper body slightly forward. Her cotton blouse strained over her thrusting breasts, pulling open at her cleavage. 'But you'll have to show me what you have in mind . . .'

Richard stood before her, his arms at his sides. His eyes travelled from her face, down to her breasts, to her hips and long legs and high-heeled shoes; then swept back up again. An impish grin spread across his face. He said throatily, 'There's nothing like rude food to give you an *appetite*.'

'So a friend of mine once told me. But I wouldn't know.' Delicious anticipation heated her sex. Shannon could not stop herself shifting from one foot to the other. The slight abrasion of her cotton panties against her labia sent shivers of pleasure through her skin. Her legs began to feel rubbery at the knees. She challenged him: 'You don't dare do it, Richard – you don't dare eat your lunch off me . . .'

'Watch me.' Richard stepped up close to her. She could not have moved away from the counter now with his body in the way, even if she had wanted to. Shannon was aware that he was reaching past her with one hand. His other hand moved towards the cleavage of her shirt.

'Let's start with dessert,' he said.

With one finger, he hooked the front of her white blouse again. Shannon looked down. Her shirt and bra were pulled forward and open. She could see the smooth globes of her breasts, skin flushed freckle-red with arousal. Her brown nipples stiffened and jutted.

Shannon looked up. In his free hand, Richard now held a tall glass full of chocolate dessert from the cool shelves behind her. Her stomach thumped. It was a wide, fluted crystal glass, holding a pint or more of cold liquid chocolate.

His thighs pressed against hers, trapping her back against the tray counter. Shannon wriggled her bum against the solid pressure. She couldn't back up. She kept her hands behind her.

'You don't dare . . .' she repeated softly.

Richard Stanley smiled. His eyes were brilliant in the rainy half-light. His face flushed, and his

183

breathing quickened. She saw him look down the front of her blouse and felt him pull the fabric tautly out and open. With his other hand he brought the dessert glass between them. Drops of condensation beaded the cool glass. The surface of the thick chocolate quivered as his hand trembled. Slowly, keeping his eyes fixed on hers, he poised the glass over her cleavage and began to tip it up.

No going back now . . . Shannon stood there, in her work suit and crisp white cotton blouse, completely motionless. The chocolate mousse dessert flowed to the lip of the glass, built up – and poured. A thick dollop of cold mousse dropped into the front of her blouse, landing with a soft, splat in the division between her breasts.

'*Oh!*' Cold, glutinous liquid shocked her hot skin. She stared down, not moving a muscle. Richard up-ended the mousse glass with one smooth movement. A pint of chilled liquid chocolate poured down her shirt, filling the front of her bra, sliding over her skin, staining the white cotton. Carefully he shifted his finger and tugged one bra-cup away from her skin. He tipped half the contents of another glass into that cup, let go, and filled her other bra cup with the remaining half. Then his finger slid out, releasing her blouse.

Wet cotton fabric slapped back against her hot, swelling breasts. Shannon gasped. She stared down at the front of her blouse, bulging full with chilled mousse, just as Richard cupped both his hands, and slapped one over each breast. Glutinous cold liquid exploded inside her shirt, plastering her skin.

'Oh . . .' she moaned as he pressed the soaking cloth against her breasts. Her nipples stung as they

184

jutted, painfully hard. Floods of pleasure pulsed in her sex. His broad, strong hands kneaded and pushed, sliming the cool chocolate over her breasts and belly. Shannon's head arched back. She bit her lip to keep from crying out.

His strong fingers grabbed the sides of her blouse and ripped. Buttons popped off and pinged away on the tile floor. The slimy wet cloth was ripped away, leaving her naked from the waist up. She glimpsed his blond hair as his head dipped, then his mouth fastened on her right breast, licking and sucking. His lips kissed delicately at the sensitive underside of her breast, now uncovered. He nibbled up to her nipple, eating off the rich dark chocolate covering the swelling nub of flesh.

She grabbed at his shoulders, knotting the cloth of his shirt in her fists. His eyes shut, his lips and face smeared brown with chocolate, he rasped his tongue from her belly to the base of her throat, licking, sucking, building a rhythm, eating her all up. Her skin shivered, quivered under cold mousse and fiery-hot tongue until her head swam with loss of control. He closed his mouth around her cream-smeared left breast, sucking the flesh in hard until his mouth was stuffed full. His tongue swirled around her nipple, flicking it to total arousal. He drew his head back, lips pulling her flesh, eating her clean, until his teeth closed around her nipple.

'Oh yes!' Shannon threw back her head, her thighs loosening, held up only by the tray-shelf behind her. His teeth nipped, once, hard, on her nipple. She spasmed in a paroxysm of pleasure, sex untouched, coming just from the feeling of thick cold chocolate licked from her breasts, and the stab of pleasure from her nipple to her sex. 'Oh, yessss . . .'

Richard lifted his head as she came. His arms, behind her now, held her up. Shannon watched him look down at her: a woman in smart ivory silk jacket and skirt, the front of her blouse ripped open, the cotton blouse and the silk jacket plastered with smears of liquid chocolate. She was flushed hot red from throat to breast.

Shannon's heaving breath quietened, slowly.

She held Richard's gaze deliberately and brought her hands around from behind her. Very casually, she reached out and pulled the waistband of his suit-trousers out a little way from his body.

Richard Stanley's hidden rod pushed out the fabric of his trousers. Under her gaze, he squirmed. 'Fair's fair,' he said thickly.

Shannon watched his crotch appreciatively. Her untouched sex craved his thick cock. But not yet . . . She smiled. 'You fill your Calvin Kleins very nicely. But let's see if I can fill your pants better . . .'

Richard frowned. 'What do you mean?'

Turning, Shannon picked up a gâteau from the cold cabinet behind her. The weight of it required two hands. It was a thick, chilled concoction of cream, chocolate and jam, eight inches across and all of five inches deep. She balanced it on the palm of one hand, weighing it thoughtfully.

'Welcome to dessert,' she said.

With one hand she pulled the waistband of his trousers and pants forward. Richard stood in front of her, arms hanging by his sides. He whispered, 'Do it . . .'

She yanked the front of his trousers forward,

186

flipped the gâteau over and plunged it down the front of his underpants. She let his waistband snap back. A little cream and jam oozed over it.

Richard stared down at the immense bulge in the front of his trousers. 'Shit, that's cold!'

Shannon met Richard's blue gaze. She flattened her palm and took careful aim. He licked his lips painfully, his aroused body completely still, not moving a muscle.

Shannon smacked her hand squarely into the middle of the bulging crotch in front of her. There was a loud squelch. She felt the gâteau explode. Cold cream, chocolate and jam filled his pants. She wiped her hands over his wet sticky crotch and fly, then grabbed his cock through the soaking, smeared cloth.

'Oh God!' he yelped. His eyes flew wide open. 'Oh Jesus, Shannon!'

Slowly, deliberately, she smeared the cold creamy mess over his belly, thighs and cock inside his trousers. Then she slowly sank down onto her knees in front of him. One hand went up and yanked down the zip of his trousers. She heard him moan. Her other hand yanked down his wet trousers and underpants together, tangling them around his knees.

'Oh please,' he whimpered, far above her, 'oh please . . .'

His erect cock bobbed in front of her face, bulbous purple tip and red thick shaft smeared in cream and chocolate. She grasped it firmly with one hand.

Richard gasped.

Slowly she lowered her mouth and licked his cock from tip to root. Sweetness burst on her tongue. She took another slow lick, as if he were an ice-cream cone, sliding her tongue around his glans. The heavy bitter-sweetness of chocolate tantalised her tastebuds. Pursing her lips, she mouthed tiny amounts of cream from his hot, hard, rigid rod. Somewhere above her, his voice whimpered in agonised anticipation. Shannon laid the whole length of her tongue along the big vein under the head of his cock, and licked, licking up, licking the glans clean and shiny and throbbing uncontrollably.

'Oh, yes!' Richard gasped.

'I'm going to eat you all up . . .' Shannon pressed her face into his sticky pubic hair. She slid her lips lower, over rough hair and the soft, smooth, hot skin of his inner thigh. She took one of his dangling balls into her mouth, twirling delicately with her tongue. His scrotum tautened instantly. She felt his hands grab her shoulders.

Shannon put her arms around his thighs as he stood spread-legged, to steady herself. She pressed her naked breasts against his legs.

'Yummy . . .' she said, lifting her head, licking cream off the scented skin of his inner thigh. He smelled of sweat, sex, and pre-come liquid. A dab of cream still smeared his lower belly where his rod jutted up archingly rigid. Above her, he groaned. She whispered, 'Yummy, sweet thing . . .'

Shannon slowly ran her tongue across his stomach, eating away the cream. His solid cock prodded under her chin, damp against her fine skin.

'Suck me,' he groaned, 'oh God, suck me!'

Obediently Shannon cupped her hands around his balls, bringing them out from between his legs, gently manipulating. She teased his stiff cock with flicks of her tongue, darting in, licking him in hot stabs. His bobbing engorged cock swelled, his velvet skin licked clean, his rod jutting up to his belly, hard as a rock. Shannon eased up on her knees and licked it, swallowing and smiling.

His hands on her shoulders clenched until it was almost painful; she would have bruises to show. '*Now!*'

She clamped her hands on his buns, digging her fingers into his muscled buttocks, her nails dragging sharply at his cool skin. He moaned.

'Now,' she said thickly. Slowly she slid her lips over the tip of his cock, taking it deeper and deeper into her mouth. Her tongue swirled, stroking and caressing the wet-hot fiery skin of his shaft. She felt it begin to swell, filling her mouth, stretching her lips. She pressed down, ringing the shaft, and slid her mouth up and down, up and down, increasing speed, hearing his moan, faster, faster, hot wet tongue lathering saliva on the bulging veins of the shaft of his throbbing cock, faster, faster—

His cock exploded in her mouth. As he came, she clamped his crotch to her face, swallowing, swallowing, eating him all, drinking him dry, until his clenched buttocks relaxed, his hands fell from her shoulders, and he swayed, barely able to stand on his feet.

'Sweet, sweet thing . . .' she murmured, wrapping her arms around him. Their sweat-hot skin clung, slicked by fiery wetness.

Her rapid breathing slowed.

She sat back and gazed up at him, the lean fair-haired man standing with his eyes shut, swaying, the front of his trousers hanging open around his knees. His big spent cock hung at half-mast. She reached up and stroked it from root to tip, with a fingertip, hardly touching, light as air. An aftershock of pleasure feathered his skin.

'Oh shit,' he breathed, 'oh shit . . . oh wow . . .'

Shannon got slowly to her feet. She felt distinctly wobbly. One of her sandals had fallen off. She stood, unbalanced, on one heel and one stockinged foot. She smiled wickedly at Richard Stanley, his flushed face and mussed hair and ruined suit trousers; all his poise lost in the overwhelming flood of pleasure she had put him through.

'I think you drained me dry . . .' He opened his eyes in time to catch her expression of disappointment. 'Don't fret,' he added. 'I'm an imaginative guy.'

'Surprise me,' Shannon said.

'I think I can do that.'

Rain rattled hard on the glass of the high windows. The strip lighting had gone off when the klaxon sounded. Now they stood in the empty café in a bright twilight, light gleaming off tiles, blond wood and the steel of the display cabinets. Delius still threaded softly through the air. Shannon licked her lips, tasting rich chocolate and sex.

She stood quite still as Richard Stanley reached out and pulled her open jacket sharply down around her shoulders. It stuck, the sleeves trapping her arms against her sides. Her bare breasts, exposed to his gaze, began to swell and flush. Her naked skin felt like electric velvet. She met his hot blue gaze.

He promised, 'I'm going to make you come like never before.'

With one twist of his strong hands, he spun

Shannon about. Now she was facing the dessert display cabinet, the tray-shelf pushing hard against the front of her thighs. A display of gâteaux and chocolate éclairs was laid out in front of her, side by side, packing all the space.

His flat hand hit her between the shoulder-blades. Helpless to put her arms out, Shannon fell face-forward, down onto the flat surface. Her belly smacked into a coffee-cream gâteaux, squelching across the front of her raw-silk skirt. Her breasts squashed flat on a big silver tray of éclairs – cream squirted between them, and out from under her. Her face plunged into a blackberry cheesecake.

'Oooooh!' She couldn't lift herself up, couldn't move. Her bottom wriggled and her legs thrashed, feet off the floor, trying to get a purchase. All that did was roll her from side to side in the creamy sugary mess. She huffed out a mouthful of cream. Sticky cheesecake clotted her face, clumping in her curls. Her bare breasts and silk-covered belly writhed in a sticky, freezing mass that now covered the top of the display cabinet.

His broad hand clamped over her buttocks, pinning her completely motionless. Shannon almost came in her knickers. She jerked her shoulders, trying to free her arms from her jacket sleeves, but it was hopeless. His other hand wiped her face free of the clinging sticky mass of black-berry jam. She opened her eyes to see there was a mirror at the back of the display case. In it, she saw Richard Stanley looking down at her. His face was flushed.

'Now . . .' he murmured. He reached down behind her, and Shannon felt him pull at the hips of her skirt, rucking it up. His strong fingers closed over the hem, and he jerked it up. The lined silk skirt tore, riding up to her waist, exposing her knickers, garter belt, and fine stockings. He stroked the crotch of her cotton panties with one light finger. Shannon's body jerked. His finger pressed in against the wet gusset of her panties. She writhed in the mess of éclairs and gâteaux, trying to thrust her fanny up to him.

Watching in the mirror, she saw him very carefully take the waistband of her white cotton panties between his fingers and thumbs, at each hip, and peel them down over her buttocks. His nails grazed the sensitive skin of her hips. Her whole body jolted with heightened sensation.

Cool air slid over her naked, clean, exposed skin.

Her breasts, flattened against a cold silver tray, swelled with arousal, sliding and smearing in cream as she attempted to roll over. No use . . .

In the mirror, she saw him haul his pants up, turn, and walk away across the café.

'Richard!'

'I said I was imaginative.'

She watched as he stopped beside the salad display. He ignored the plates. He murmured, 'Are you an appetiser? Or is this you getting your just deserts?'

She saw him reach out. In the decorative display of fruit and vegetables, kept chilled so that they would remain fresh for the day, there was a smooth-skinned green cucumber. Richard Stanley picked it up. It was eight or nine inches long – and *thick*, Shannon saw; his hand would hardly close around its girth.

'Sorry I have to let you down,' he said as he

walked back towards her. 'But my friend here should *more* than satisfy you . . .'

As he came up behind her, she found herself staring at her reflection in the mirror. The mirror exposed a prone woman, dressed in the suit and skirt of a sharp executive, her smart jacket and blouse covered in dark chocolate and thick cream; her hair sweaty and messy, her face red with the flush of arousal. Light gleamed from her pale, raised, naked buttocks.

Shannon squirmed on her belly in the mess. 'I can take whatever you dish out,' Shannon promised.

His hand vanished from her view. She couldn't help it, her hips jerked. A finger trailed down the curve of her buttock, brushing the outermost damp hairs of her cleft. Her clitoris throbbed. Her flesh ran with juices, and she moaned deep in her throat.

'Do it!' she moaned. 'Right up me!'

In the mirror, she saw his flushed face. His limp cock, hanging out of his pants, twitched and began to swell. He dropped his free hand to his crotch. As his cock began to come erect again, he lifted his other hand into view, letting her see the thick, thick girth of the cucumber.

His knee prodded her thighs roughly apart.

'I want you to be really ready,' his voice said.

Shannon raised her head. He had picked up a cream cake. As she watched in the mirror, he held it poised above her naked buttocks. She wriggled, spreading her legs, and shut her eyes.

'Ooohh!' A sudden squelch, and the cream cake hit her squarely between the legs; cold and smooth and creamy over her sex. His hand smeared it right up her. She hardly needed lubrication, juices flowed from her already, hot and wet. 'Fill me!'

She had little time to prepare – a thick, chilled tip prodded at the soaking outer lips of her labia. Then, without warning, his strong wrist thrust. The whole length of a thick, solid, freezing-cold object thrust straight up Shannon's sex.

'Oh!' She gasped. Her whole body froze, utterly still. The icy fullness stretched her almost unbearably. Big as it was, her arousal had made her ready for it. The shock of hard cold vegetable in wet, hot skin made her shudder with pleasure. Still, she dared not move her hips. She sprawled flat, bent over the counter, face down in cream, her sex stuffed to its fullest.

Gently, gradually, he began to thrust, withdraw, thrust, withdraw . . .

'Oh God!' Her skin flushed red from foot to neck. Her nipples jammed hard against the silver tray. She rolled her upper body from side to side, smearing her breasts with cold cream and chocolate sauce. Her legs strained, and she heard the hem of her skirt rip as she spread her thighs open even wider. The hard cold slickness shoved up into her soaking hot sex, teasing her, filling her.

Sweat poured from her face, slicked her breasts, stained the raw silk jacket. In the mirror she saw Richard draw his arm back for the final thrust. His other hand rubbed furiously at his crotch.

'Yes,' she yelled, 'yes, *yes*!'

'Take it!' Smoothly, unstoppably, Richard thrust the whole thick length up inside her. The chilly, blunt rounded end pushed her flesh apart. The muscles of her vagina spasmed against it, hot against cold. The whole length of it shoved her aroused flesh apart, thrust her wide, triggering an explosive convulsion deep in her belly.

She spasmed uncontrollably. Her sex shuddered, and flooded. Richard, with a loud groan, fell forward over her bum as he ejaculated across the backs of her stockinged legs.

'Oh *yes!*'

Shannon came thunderously.

The security alert was over by four in the afternoon. The guards hardly thought it worth opening up again, but orders came down from above. Frank Simmons opened up the lower galleries, and the café.

He nodded sociably in passing to two of the kitchen staff in their distinctive white overalls. A man and a woman, both carrying bin-bags; probably taking them out to the rubbish disposal unit, he thought.

If he had been a little less weary with his unsuccessful search of the building, he might have wondered why both of them had glistening damp clean hair. Why would the catering staff wash their hair in the kitchens, after all?

Frank Simmons was far too annoyed to think about it.

The last thing he heard, as he turned away towards the Egyptian Gallery, was the woman speaking to the man.

Her voice floated down the corridor.

'I may have misjudged you, Richard. You really must ask me out for lunch again sometime . . .'

Chapter Twelve

August 29th.

  Shannon Garrett stood at her office window, gazing down.

Last Friday of the month. . .

Why didn't we get any bets on Thursday? Today?

Time's up, now.

Beyond the glass, the last drops of a lashing grey storm drummed on the window. Shannon, in the warmth of her office, under yellow strip-lighting, stared at rainy morning twilight outside. Gone 9 a.m. . . .

  And not a word from upstairs yet! *Why?*

Across the rain-lashed expanse of concrete, six floors below, a tiny figure holding a mac over its head made a dash for the building's main entrance. Shannon turned away from the window.

'Lisa, any chance of two coffees – no, make that two hot chocolates?'

'Sure.' Lisa, Julia Royston's young assistant, regarded Shannon anxiously from outside the tiny office. 'I don't suppose you've heard anything about us? The MD hasn't said whether it's us or *Babes!*?'

There were a number of covert listeners attending, Shannon noticed: Gary fiddling with his earring and pretending to study his workstation monitor, Julia correcting a typescript by hand and sucking furiously at one lock of her dark red hair, even young Mike making a great production of signing for an envelope to go across town . . .

'Not a word.' Shannon heard a familiar voice out at the reception desk. 'You know I'll tell everybody the minute I hear something. Chocolate in my office, thanks. Alix, hello.'

'Hi, boss.' The young woman strode between the workstations, trailing a soaking jade-green mac. Her tied-back silver hair was wind-blown, tangled, and wet. 'Don't suppose you've got a towel handy, have you?'

Several minutes and some borrowed kitchen towel later, Shannon sat at her desk opposite a considerably drier Alix Neville. The young woman untangled and brushed her long hair and let it hang loose about her shoulders to dry off completely. She reached for her mug of hot chocolate and drank deeply.

'Nothing?' Alix licked a moustache of brown chocolate from her upper lip, her grey eyes troubled. 'No,' she answered her own question, 'or you would have said. *Why* haven't we heard . . . ?' A pause. 'Shannon, there's something I want to say here. I guess you won't like it.'

'Go ahead.' Shannon sat back. It might well be the case that everything in the tiny cubicle was within her arm's reach without moving out of the chair, but it was still her office, her magazine now, and she ached when she thought of losing it all.

Alix, her wet shoes kicked off, stockinged feet curled up under her, and long hair down around her face, seemed very young. 'What it is . . .' Alix paused. 'It isn't *fair*.'

'Go on.' Shannon kept her voice non-committal.

'It's also a draw,' the young woman said, her voice suddenly sharp and dry. 'They did everything we did, we did everything they did – *and* enjoyed it. Who's won the bet?'

Shannon sighed. 'As far as I can see – no one!'

'Exactly!' Alix thumped her empty mug down on top of the previous month's copy of *Femme*, the one with the handsome black woman on the cover. 'Vince is a bit of a sweetie.' Her voice held a laugh, not far under the surface. 'Not that he'd want to be told that! But he is. And you should see him in action . . .'

Alix's expression went momentarily vague. Then her gaze snapped back to Shannon and she grinned.

'Yeah, you really ought to see him! He's quite something. And – listen – I know you don't like him, but Richard's quite something, too. That boy is a *machine*.' The young woman looked serious. '*And* I know you don't believe me, but – underneath all that shit he hands out, Richard's actually a nice guy.'

'Really?' Shannon covered her mouth with her hand, stifling a smile of her own. 'Perhaps – underneath – he's got hidden depths. And a few surprises.'

Alix's grey eyes gleamed. She leaned forward, almost falling off the office chair. '*Really* . . . ?'

Shannon looked innocently at her. 'Richard and

I had lunch on Wednesday, while you were at your conference.'

'Oh.' Alix sank back on the chair. She brushed curls of silver hair back out of her face. 'I thought you meant something *interesting*.'

'He has an interesting way with vegetables,' Shannon offered.

'So he cooked for you. Big deal.'

'You might like his *Cucumber Surprise*. It's very filling.'

'I ain't no vegetarian,' Alix grumbled. 'I've never understood what people see in vegetables. Shannon, what *is* the matter?'

'Nothing!' Shannon bit the inside of her lip, hard. It didn't work. She whooped out loud, and clapped her hands over her mouth. In the outer office, Julia Royston turned around and stared. Shannon pretended a ferocious interest in her workstation monitor.

'*Sha*nnon . . .'

'And you wouldn't believe what he can do with a dessert.' The sight of Alix Neville's completely bemused expression sent Shannon off into stifled paroxysms of laughter. 'Sorry . . . ! Sometimes life just hands you a straight line.'

'Well, it's handing you a lemon today. Us, or Richard Stanley.'

Alix's flat tone brought her down to earth.

'That's right. Us or them; me or Richard . . .' Shannon's amusement faded. 'I tell you what, Alix, even if we do get a final bet today – this is a bloody *stupid* way to decide this!'

Alix nodded enthusiastically. 'That's exactly what I was trying to say!'

'I don't want Richard to lose his job,' Shannon

continued. 'I don't want to lose mine. I don't want my staff made redundant. But if the company's going to do it, they might at least give us the dignity of doing it for a reason. *Let* the accountants decide! This isn't fair.'

Alix seized and threw a stack of papers into the air.

'Yeah!' she whooped. 'That's what I hoped you'd say! Shannon, call Edmund Howard – *tell him the bet's off.*'

Sheets of computer print-out dropped onto desk, floor, and Shannon Garrett indiscriminately. She pushed a concertina of paper off her lap. 'That'll solve the problem, okay! As soon as I tell Edmund Howard the bet's off, my redundancy notice goes in his Out Tray . . . But this *isn't* fair. And I'm going to say so. Come on!'

Shannon stood up.

Startled, Alix Neville tried unsuccessfully to shove her damp stockinged feet back into her high-heeled shoes. 'Where are we going?'

'The penthouse floor,' Shannon said grimly. 'Somehow I don't think we'll have to make an appointment. Come on . . .'

As she walked into the penthouse's anteroom, Alix at her heels, Shannon came to a sudden halt. Richard Stanley was sitting on one of the charcoal-upholstered chairs – and Vince Russell was with him.

She had a second to look at Richard's bowed head, the fine fluff of blond hair growing on the nape of his strong neck. Then he glanced up and got rapidly to his feet. He was wearing a steel-grey suit and slate-grey tie, his nails manicured and clean; and the scent of his cologne drifted across the anteroom to her. All smartened up for an interview with the MD . . . Shannon couldn't stop her eyes drifting down the triangular sweep of his shoulders, chest and waist, to the well-fitting crotch of his trousers.

Beside him, Vince Russell also stood up. A tall man, a *big* man; his uniform jacket rain-spotted, smelling warm and damp. His brown eyes went past Shannon, to Alix. He hooked his thumbs in his uniform belt, boots planted squarely apart. Alix rested her small, strong hand on Shannon's arm, wriggling her foot into her shoe at last, ignoring the big man completely.

Shannon opened her mouth to speak. Edmund Howard's PA looked up from his desk, thumbed a button, and stood. 'If you'd like to come this way, Mr Howard is ready to see you now.'

Alix, beside her, gave a little shrug. Shannon Garrett stood back to let the two men precede her into Edmund Howard's private office, thinking furiously, *What's going on here?*

The floor-length windows in the big room gleamed with watery sunlight. Twenty floors above Canary Wharf, high enough now to see the last veils of rain sweeping across the Thames, fading into grey over the City.

Edmund Howard was seated at his desk, his back to the windows. Shannon squinted into the growing sunlight, unable to make out his expression.

'Take a seat,' his voice directed.

'Sir.' Richard Stanley moved forward past the low table and leather sofa, towards the upright wing-armed walnut chairs in front of the desk. Then he hesitated, glanced back, and pulled out a

201

chair for Shannon. Her eyebrows lifted, but she walked forward and seated herself; Richard beside her. Alix took a seat next to her, and the ex-army security man took a seat next to Richard.

Shannon looked across Edmund Howard's bare expanse of desk and said bluntly, 'We were expecting a bet yesterday. Sir. What happened?'

'If I may—?' Beside her, Richard Stanley interrupted. He sat bolt upright in his chair. The polished wood surface of the desk in front of him reflected his pale features and neat blond hair. Shannon saw he had a slight sheen of sweat on his forehead. 'Sir?'

There was a moment's silence. Edmund Howard's chill, resonant voice said, 'Proceed, Mr Stanley.'

'Before you give us another bet – there's something I'd like to say. To register a protest.' Richard Stanley abandoned formality. 'I don't think Shannon and her people deserve to have their future decided this way!'

Another silence: this one very chill. Beyond the rain-wet glass, watery sunlight began to spread over the tower-blocks of Canary Wharf.

'And you, Ms Garrett? You have something to say?'

Now that the room became brighter, Shannon could make out the black silhouette of the Managing Director more clearly: Edmund Howard's grey wool Savile Row suit, and the glint of the expensive watch on his wrist. Growing sunlight illuminated his razor-cut silver hair. His face was still invisible.

'Yes. I do. I agree. I don't think *Richard*'s magazine's future should be decided this way. This isn't right.' Shannon rubbed one hand through her ruffled red-brown curls. 'Mr Howard – I think *you* think so too. Or we would have heard from this office yesterday.'

'Do you, indeed?' Edmund Howard rose to his feet. He turned and walked to the window of his office, surveying the dispersing clouds. The light fell on his deeply creased face, his shaggy silver brows. The strengthening sun gleamed on his erect back. Shannon, if she had not known him to be in his sixties, would have thought him a decade younger.

When he turned back to them, Shannon caught unexpected humour in his bright blue gaze. 'I don't like to lose a bet either, Ms Garrett. I resent the fact that I shall have to tell my colleagues that they were right – that this is not a viable economic method of choosing between two newsstand titles. That grieves me. Nonetheless, you are correct, Ms Garrett. I have decided to call off the bets.'

Beside Shannon, Alix Neville stirred in her seat. '*We*—'

Shannon kicked her ankle smartly.

'I have handed the paperwork for both *Femme* and *Babes!* over to the accounts people this morning. It is now irrevocably out of my hands,' Edmund Howard concluded, resting those gnarled, powerful hands on the back of his chair. His amazingly blue eyes swept across the four of them. 'Unfortunately, Accounts state that they require more data to work with; a final decision will therefore not be possible until the end of this year. I regret that you and your staff will have to wait four months longer for the final decision. There is now nothing I can do about that.'

A flood of anti-climax swept through Shannon's body, leaving her limp and weak with reaction. *So that's it – that's final. . .*

Alix Neville reached up, her green silk shirt-dress stretching taut across her breasts; she swept her tumbling mass of hair together between her hands and fastened it up with a black scrunchie. Her elfin features were expressionless. Richard placed his palms on his lean muscular thighs, about to push himself up from his chair. Beyond him, the big crop-haired man slumped: Vince Russell sagging in his seat.

'I'm sorry it will be necessary for me to lose any of you,' Edmund Howard added. 'I may say that you are – all – remarkably imaginative and talented. It's a great shame. Ladies and gentlemen, thank you.' He reached for the small panel set into the boardroom table, and his PA's call-button.

Well, that's it. Now there isn't anything *any* of us can do, not even him. It's over. Back to being mundane. No more excitement . . .

No, damn it! Shannon thought. There's one thing I've always wanted to do – but I didn't want to do it while there was still a decision to be made . . .

'Sir.' Shannon didn't move from her chair. 'I don't believe you've had a full report. Shouldn't you debrief us verbally?'

'I believe I do have full reports.' Edmund Howard's sharp blue gaze rested on her. 'You will recall, Ms Garrett, that I have the CCTV footage from the mall, the gymnasium, Madam Natalie's establishment – and,' he added, 'the Midnight Rose International building's car park . . .'

Vince Russell's head lowered like a bull. His

stubbled skin flushed. Richard Stanley busied himself adjusting the buttoned cuffs of his crisp white shirt.

'But,' Shannon said' 'I don't think you have footage of my car service with Donna – she's a mechanic. Or my . . . interesting . . . lunch with Richard. Or Alix's photo-shoot with Mr Stanley. . .'

She felt her throat tighten, her mouth go dry, keeping eye-contact with the intimidating older man. Edmund Howard took his hand away from the call button.

'Your extra-curricular activities?' The creases of his face deepened in a smile. Edmund Howard fixed a direct gaze on Shannon. Her belly jumped, a pulse of adrenaline running through her veins.

'I do have my sources,' the powerful old man said quietly. 'Perhaps it isn't surprising that I have access to the photo studio's after-hours footage of Ms Neville. It took me rather more effort to get American security footage of Mr Stanley from my West Coast office.'

Shannon heard distinct winces behind her. Edmund Howard moved around his desk until he stood in front of Shannon. She gazed up at him.

'Sadly, no record exists of your visit to your garage,' he said softly, 'or your – museum visit. It seems that in the latter case, the camera systems failed during the power-cut.'

Shannon felt her cheeks reddening. She didn't look at Richard. A breathlessness tightened her chest. *Am I glad or sorry?*

Shannon stood up. Edmund Howard was a good six inches taller than her. She noted the breadth of his chest now that she was standing so close to him. If he wore cologne, it was discreet; her nostrils flared to the faint male scent from his expensively dressed body. The light from the window gleamed on his silver hair, and his creased, lined, *used* face. His blue eyes, meeting hers, held a depth of sophisticated humour and experience.

Shannon brought her high-heeled black shoes together. Her charcoal suit skirt came just above her knees now that she was on her feet, and her jacket, flared at the hip, was buttoned neatly in front over her snowy blouse. The picture of a female executive . . .

'What a shame that I missed it all,' Edmund Howard rumbled. 'I think you would have been one of the most – entertaining – members of my staff.'

'I haven't finished yet.' Shannon turned on her heel. She faced Alix Neville. The young woman still had the dampness of rain darkening the shoulders of her jade-green silk shirt-dress. Pearl buttons gleamed, half-hidden by her mass of silver hair. Shannon's gaze fixed on the shadowed warm cleft between Alix's full breasts. She put one finger out to touch the next button down.

'You said something to me when this started.' Shannon raised her eyes to the young woman's elfin face. 'Remember?'

Alix met her gaze. 'I said, if there was a bet involving a woman, I'd come and see my boss . . .'

Shannon's attention narrowed down until she could see only the tall young woman. She was aware of Edmund Howard's hawk-gaze raking her back; but Richard's wide-open mouth and Vince Russell's stare faded into the background.

'How about I show our Managing Director what

he's been missing?' Shannon murmured.

Alix Neville reached out. Her slender, strong fingers undid the button of Shannon's executive jacket. 'Why don't you show *me* what *I've* been missing?'

With one swift movement, Shannon shrugged her jacket off and threw it on to the carpet. The new sun blazed back from Alix's tangled, still-drying silver mass of curls. Shannon stepped up close and slid her fingers into the young woman's hair, smoothing it back from her face. The pads of her fingers tingled, brushing Alix's warm temples.

Shannon dropped her hands to the front of Alix's dress. Her fingers shook. She undid one pearl button, and the green silk began to gape. A deep cleft of warm flesh became visible. The younger woman was not wearing a bra, Shannon realised; Alix's little nipples hardened and stood out clearly under the silk.

Her own nipples stiffened. In her groin, warmth flowered; skirt and pantyhose abruptly constricting.

'There . . .' Shannon drew the dress apart. Silky material strained over full round globes of flesh. She bared Alix's breasts. The open dress hung, buttoned only at the hem now, gaping to show slender torso, tiny navel, and the flare of her narrow hips. Lace-trimmed green satin knickers clung to the young woman's smooth skin.

Shannon bent her head and tongued Alix's nipple lightly. The brown nub protruded, stiffening. A tiny moan crept from between the younger woman's full lips. She lowered her silver lashes, hands at her sides. Shannon cupped her hands and grabbed a breast in each hand and squeezed.

'Oh!' Alix's eyes flew wide open.

'I've wanted to do this for a long time ...' Shannon, without loosening her grip, walked the young woman backwards to the leather sofa. Its arm caught Alix behind her knees. She fell back, sprawling, the last button ripping open on her dress. Shannon fell with her.

Shannon shot a glance over her shoulder. Edmund Howard stood behind his desk, his hands on the back of his chair. The light of the summer morning meant she could no longer read his expression.

Slowly Shannon began to unbutton her own blouse. Richard Stanley stared at her, open-mouthed. She stifled a giggle. His face was shocked – but his fine-haired, lean hand had crept down to the crotch of his trousers. He gripped himself as she watched.

Shannon peeled off her blouse. Her breasts flushed in her black satin bra. Alix stretched and curled like a cat, silver hair all over her face, her back arching, her bare breasts thrust up.

'Oh God!' Shannon's sex pulsed wetly. Before she could move, the younger woman knelt up on the sofa and stuffed her hand down the front of Shannon's skirt. Her strong small fingers wiggled under Shannon's pantyhose, dug down her belly, under her knickers, and plunged into her hot cleft.

'I can make you come,' Alix said breathlessly. 'I can. Can't I, Vince?'

She spoke without looking over her shoulder at the burly security man. Shannon found she was facing him. His expression was thunderstruck. The front of his uniform trousers bulged.

Shannon clapped her hand over Alix's, pushing

it deeper into her cleft. With her other hand she grabbed Alix's body, pressing it to her, pressing her bare, slick, hot breasts against her own. She felt Alix's hand come up her back, flick her bra fastening undone. She sprawled across Alix, bare belly to bare belly, on the leather sofa.

Hands were at her waist, Alix wrenching her tight skirt open. Shannon writhed, jerking her legs, ripping the hem right up the back. Her loosened bra fell off. She struggled out of her hose and knickers. Alix's hands grabbed her breasts, kneading and squeezing and pinching at her nipples. She wound her legs around the young woman's waist, pinning her, and bent to lick her tongue right across Alix's hot, sweet, salty-tasting collarbone. Her labia swelled and throbbed.

A small, strong hand thrust three fingers up inside her.

'Ooohhh!' Shannon gritted her teeth. Her hands closed tightly on Alix's breasts. The young woman gasped. Shannon began to squeeze and relax, squeeze and relax. Kneeling over Alix on the sofa, she spread her thighs wide. The fingers plunged into her wet, running sex; delicious friction searing her with pleasure.

Shannon gazed down.

Both Alix's hands were at her thighs now, one gripping hard, one thrusting up. Sparkles of pleasure danced across Shannon's vision. She pressed down, closing her fingers, and the pale flesh of Alix's breasts squeezed up between them.

'Oh, yes!' Alix's head thrashed, sweat-wet silver hair flying. Her green satin knickers pulled tight across her crotch as she writhed. Shannon saw the young woman's hard little clit poking at the front of her pants.

She leaned, taking the silky satin cloth between her teeth, and dragged it down over Alix's hips.

'Now!' Shannon plunged her face down, fastening her mouth on Alix's clit, sucking and licking, writhing her wet, hot tongue around the hard nub of flesh. Alix's body arched, ecstatically, almost throwing her off, and the young woman came, her juices flooding down Shannon's throat and breasts.

As Alix came, Shannon felt her slam her fingers up. 'Yes!' The fingers stiffened, thrust furiously, and Shannon rode them, her body arching up off the leather sofa, coming with every thrust of Alix's hard, slender, strong young hand.

Shannon bent to kiss Alix. Then she scrambled up from the sofa, leaving the dishevelled young woman to kneel upright and gaze in bright-eyed amazement. Completely naked, Shannon Garrett paced across the carpeted floor, in the warm sunlight.

She took hold of the back of Richard Stanley's trousers.

'What?'

Shannon reached around his hot, slightly sweating body, and undid his trouser belt.

'But—' Richard protested as his pants fell to the floor.

Shannon extended the middle finger of her right hand, slid it between her drenched thighs, and jammed it straight up Richard Stanley's bottom. His anus clenched on her – and began to relax.

Shannon moved her finger gently and rhythmically in and out. His breathing roughened. From the waist up, he was all executive suit and tie. From the waist down, Richard Stanley stood naked, being finger-fucked by the woman behind him.

Out of the corner of her eye, Shannon saw Alix Neville, naked, her hair falling down to her flushed hips, pad past the desk.

Alix put both hands on her hips, facing Edmund Howard.

'Don't you think,' she said, the gurgle of a laugh in her voice, 'that you ought to try us out for yourself, sir? After all, all you've had so far are other people's reports . . .'

Shannon could only see his silhouette at the window. The older man's body was smartly upright, apparently unmoved by what he was watching.

'I hardly feel—' The MD's powerful voice cracked.

'Oh God!' Richard Stanley's bum clamped tight shut on Shannon's middle finger and his hips jerked forward.

Shannon reached out for the tissue box on the desk, not taking her eyes off Alix and the MD. As she wiped her finger, she purred, 'Maybe we ought to *show* him, Alix . . .'

Alix grinned happily. 'Yeah, show no mercy, that's what I always say! You're on! Unless . . .' She turned back to face Edmund Howard. In a quite different tone, she added, 'Unless you really want us to leave . . .'

Shannon left the desk, moving around it to where she had the light from the window falling on Edmund Howard. The tall, powerful, silver-haired man stood with his fists clenched at his sides. There was a distinct bulge in his expensive, well-cut suit trousers.

'Here at Midnight Rose International, I always pride myself that my staff are thoroughly satisfied,' Edmund Howard remarked. 'Are you?'

'Not yet.' Shannon licked her lips. She stood, naked, the sun hot on the carpet under her bare feet. Her skin tingled, velvet and electric, exposed to the gaze of passing gulls and traffic helicopters. The silver-haired man gazed down at her. His manicured nails were blunt, square-cut; and his deeply worn hands large and strong. A new warmth began to throb in her groin. 'I don't know about the boys, sir, but I'm not nearly finished yet!'

Edmund Howard looked down at her with blue, sparkling eyes.

'Dear me,' he said mildly. 'I appear to have forgotten to call my PA.'

'Oh dear,' Shannon echoed. She felt a grin spread across her face. 'What a shame.'

Alix Neville walked up to stand behind Edmund Howard. 'Looks like the Managing Director's going to get fucked.'

'Help, help,' Edmund Howard remarked dryly.

The silver-haired young woman put her full lips up to his ear. 'And there's not a thing you can do about it. You've seen us in action. You're in the hands of experts . . .'

Edmund Howard's arousal grew plainer. Shannon stepped forward and closed her hand over the bulge in his trousers. Her fingers and palm encountered a stubby, short cock – with a girth that made her suddenly look down in amazement, face colouring a brilliant scarlet at what she held in her hand.

Vince Russell stepped forward from behind her. Moving startlingly fast and light for such a big man, he stepped round behind the Managing Director and locked Edmund Howard's arms behind his back.

Shannon met Vince's gaze. The brown-eyed man said harshly, 'Suck him!'

Shannon sank to her knees in front of the pinioned man. She reached up and slowly unbuttoned his trousers. She pulled the fabric down, sliding Edmund Howard's underpants down around his knees. His short cock jutted straight out at her. Reaching up, she couldn't close her hand around its hot, trembling thickness.

'Oh, man . . .' Shannon lowered her head, taking his cock into her elegant lipsticked mouth. Small strong hands wrapped around Edmund Howard's hairy thighs from the back: Alix knelt, pressing her naked boobs against his legs, sliding her hands up to part his nether cheeks, and darting her stiff pink tongue into his anus.

Above Shannon, Edmund Howard's body thrashed. He yelled something uncontrolled, unintelligible, and fought against Vince Howard's restraining grip.

Shannon took his pale, short, thick cock into her mouth; stuffing her mouth full, her lips stretching to contain him. As she slid her tongue around his pulsing glans, she watched Alix rimming him with her tongue, her fingers digging deep into his clenched buttocks. Shannon slid her wide-stretched lips up and down his shaft, matching her rhythm to Alix's thrust; smelling sweat and male cologne, wrapping her arms around his lean, strong hairy thighs, one hand going up to squeeze his scrotum—

Behind her, strong knees forced her legs wide

213

apart. She couldn't look round. Her sex stiffened, flooded. Two hands grabbed her buttocks, forcing them apart.

Alix's eyes flew wide. Shannon saw, past her naked shoulders and bouncing breasts, Vince Russell kneeling down. While one hand still gripped Edmund Howard's wrists, his other hand frigged his cock erect, and stuffed it straight up Alix Neville's hot little pussy. Vince Russell pushed, each thrust lifting the silver-haired young woman up on her knees. Alix shut her eyes, tongue still thrusting up the Managing Director's helpless ass; and Shannon saw Vince Russell clamp her firmly onto his cock with his free hand flat across her belly.

Shannon's mouth felt stuffed wide. She made her lips stiff, sliding them faster and faster up and down the incredibly thick shaft of Edmund Howard's prick. Richard Stanley, behind her, jammed his finger up her anus. A thrill of pleasure jolted her whole body. She flattened her bum and spread her thighs, mouth full, ass full, sex aching to be stuffed.

Strong hands seized her under the arms, dragging her up on to her feet, her open mouth coming off Edmund's cock. She gazed dizzily up into his lined, blue-eyed, strong face.

'I'm – impressed—' Edmund gasped. 'Now, Mr Stanley!'

Shannon felt the finger leave her bottom. Hands spread her thighs. Edmund Howard grabbed her breasts. As she gasped, he shoved his hips forward. The incredibly wide head of his cock stuffed up inside her, filling her to the brim.

Richard Stanley's hands clamped on her hips.

214

He pulled her buttocks apart. His hot cock plunged hard, straight up her ready back passage. His hard hips banged her bum, his balls bouncing up against her. Shannon yelled in ecstasy.

Clamped between the two of them, Shannon's hands went loose and her whole body slumped, dizzily, as they began simultaneously to pump her. She began to come with each thrust.

'Ohhh!' Shannon's eyes went wide. 'Oh no . . . oh God . . .'

Shannon came as she had never come before in her life, and fell forward, slumped, drained, into the slick, sweating, panting embraces of Edmund, Richard, Alix and Vince.

Chapter Thirteen

MEMO

Date: 1 January 1998
From: Edmund Howard, Managing Director
To: Accounts; Sales & Marketing; staff of *Babes!* and *Femme* magazines.
Subject: Downsizing monthly magazine titles

As you know, in view of the current economic situation it has become necessary for Midnight Rose International to downsize one of its monthly magazine titles. The titles due for reassessment over the past half-year have been *Femme* and *Babes!*.

Over the past three months, sales figures for *Babes!* have taken a positive upturn of 73%. Public response indicates this is due to a favourable response to the photo-series *CCTV SURPRISE!* which features explicit 'security scenario' footage, both genuine and that reproduced by Midnight Rose International using their own staff for the staged photo-shoots. The management has been particularly impressed by the performance of Mr V. Russell in this respect.

However, over a similar three-month period, the sales figures for *Femme* have gone up by 78%. Our reader questionnaire attributes this to the 'Dungeon-Mistress' series of articles by a new and exciting features writer, Ms A. Neville, whom we shall be employing on a punishing schedule in future.

As the most uneconomic title, *Babes!* will therefore be dropped from the Midnight Rose International conglomerate. The management extends its commiserations to the editor and staff members.

On a happier note, those of you who have been with Midnight Rose International for any length of time will be aware of the sterling work done by Theodore J. Cartwright in his forty years of editing *Classic Steam*. Mr Cartwright has recently expressed a personal wish that he be allowed to take retirement on his seventy-first birthday, in February, to spend more time with his wife and his models of the Settle-to-Carlisle line.

Midnight Rose International is happy to comply.

Since we feel that no one can adequately follow in Theodore Cartwright's footsteps as editor, *Classic Steam* will cease publication after a special forty-year retrospective February issue.

As this leaves a gap in our schedule, the management have decided to revitalise a disused title. The new erotic top-shelf photo-magazine *Voyeur* (previously *Babes!*) will be scheduled to appear from January. All *Babes!* editors and photo-staff will be retained.

Please note that the Managing Director wishes to see the following in his office as soon as possible, to discuss discipline at work:

S. Garrett
A. Neville
R. Stanley
V. Russell

Edmund Howard, MD